Great! You've Just Ruined the Rest of My Life

Yvonne Coppard is British and lives in Cambridgeshire with her husband and two children. She works as an advisory teacher (child protection), but has written several books for young adults, one of which was shortlisted for the 1990 Federation of Children's Book Groups Children's Book Award.

Other books by Yvonne Coppard

EVERYBODY ELSE DOES! WHY CAN'T I?
NOT DRESSED LIKE THAT, YOU DON'T!

Great! You've Just Ruined the Rest of My Life

Yvonne Coppard

PUFFIN BOOKS

To Mave and Jack, and all our friends in
Saanich, with thanks

PUFFIN BOOKS

Published by the Penguin Group
Penguin Books Ltd, 27 Wrights Lane, London W8 5TZ, England
Penguin Books USA Inc., 375 Hudson Street, New York, New York 10014, USA
Penguin Books Australia Ltd, Ringwood, Victoria, Australia
Penguin Books Canada Ltd, 10 Alcorn Avenue, Toronto, Ontario, Canada M4V 3B2
Penguin Books (NZ) Ltd, 182–190 Wairau Road, Auckland 10, New Zealand

Penguin Books Ltd, Registered Offices: Harmondsworth, Middlesex, England

First published by Piccadilly Press Ltd 1995
Published in Puffin Books 1996
3 5 7 9 10 8 6 4 2

Made and printed in England by Clays Ltd, St Ives plc

How am I going to survive two years of this? Some of my friends are out working. They get money, freedom, and evenings out. Me? I get hassle at school, where they still treat me like a kid, hassle at home, ditto, and poverty. They told me life in the Sixth Form would be different. They lied. I don't even know what career I want yet, so why bother? I mean, I could slog away for two years and then decide I want to work in a clothes shop, or be a wife and mother. Dad says shops and babies both require an educated approach, and the only jobs where it wouldn't be better to have qualifications are the really boring ones. That's rich, coming from him – he's got a sackful of qualifications and probably the most boring job in the world. Not even Mum can say exactly what he does – she just tells people he's 'in computers for a multi-national company'. You don't get more boring than that.

The teachers this year are not too bad, but there's one new one who is a real prat. His name's Jack J. Jackson, so even his parents must have been naff. He wears cord trousers, a baggy jacket with leather patches on the elbows (just to be a poser, though, because the jacket's new), and a stringy black leather tie. He also wears suede shoes, and talks with this weird accent. He's American, but he tries to sound English. It doesn't work, just like the jacket doesn't work. Jack J. Jackson came to England from San Francisco, U.S.A. because he felt, like, that's where his real roots were, man, know what I mean? He told us that it was pure accident that he was born an American. His soul, apparently, is British. Sadie asked him, rather nastily but none of us cared, if he understood that no person BORN in Britain would ever say they were British – they'd be English, Irish, Scots, or Welsh. He looked all confused, and then said he was 'a transitory Brit searching for the true core of his Britishness'.

I suppose he had to become a teacher of English

Literature or go into some small private institution where they lock the doors and your relatives never hear from you again. Sadie and I hate him, and feel it's a cheek to have a foreigner trying to teach us Shakespeare. He's a mega-poser; he thinks he's a real expert. We're doing Jane Austen at the moment – *Pride and Prejudice*. He gives us these long lectures which he calls 'essential background', so he can show off his knowledge. Sadie and I are well fed up of him, and we are determined to trip him up. We are spending lots of time in the library gathering information and reading ahead so that we can show off, too, and stop him treating the whole class as if he's had to travel the Atlantic to save us from our ignorance. Whenever he makes a mistake, we're there to point it out.

I didn't realize that things had got so bad in the teaching profession that the government had to dredge the bottom of the barrel like this. The man's a real fruit and nut case.

The only good part of my life is George, my gorgeous student nurse. Today is our anniversary – five weeks exactly since our first proper date.

8th October

Jenny has got stuck into her studies this year with a vengeance, especially English Lit. They have a new teacher, an American. I met him briefly at the induction evening for the Sixth Form Centre. He is mustard keen, and even dresses the part. I think he saw 'Goodbye Mr Chips' when he was a boy, and hasn't realized that the film was made decades ago and teachers have changed just a wee bit since then. But he certainly does something right. Jenny has really flourished in his class. Her room is stacked with background reading and notes for essays. I think she's developing a bit of a crush on him. He reminds me a

2

lot of Mike at his age, but I suppose that's the tie and the suede shoes... I asked Jenny about him. She spluttered and said, 'Don't mention that man's name to me,' in a rather over-the-top way, which I suppose means she does fancy him like mad. Poor Mr Jackson; it will be awkward for him being followed around by adoring adolescent schoolgirls in his first year of teaching. I think Sadie is rather taken with him, too. She and Jenny seem to spend a lot of time muttering about him. He is dishy – if I was in the market for a toy boy I could go for him myself.

Jon likes his teacher very much. Her name is Miss Treetop, and Jon adores everything about her, including her name. It is good to see Jon and Jenny both happily settled at school. Lizzie is a joy to have around. She smiles all the time, and whenever I look at her I think how lucky we are. She was a surprise, no doubt about that, and I'm not sure I would ever have chosen to have another baby at my age, so she is here by pure, blessed luck. I just wish I wasn't so tired; I feel like a very old woman, more like a granny than a mother. I don't think I can bear to go back to work, though officially I'm only on maternity leave. I have to decide what to do soon, I suppose, but it will be difficult either way. If I wait until Lizzie's in school I may well not be able to get another job at the age I'll be then, but if I go back even part-time to the hospital I feel I'll be cheated of time I want to spend with the baby. Decisions, decisions.

October 12th

George's family had a reunion this weekend. It was actually a late celebration of his sister's wedding in the Summer, which a lot of the family couldn't get to because flights were too expensive then. But George says they have a reunion at least once a year – if there's

3

nothing to celebrate then they make something up! It's quite an achievement to get everybody together, especially on his mum's side. For a start, George has a brother and five sisters; their house bursts at the seams. Then there are his other relatives, who all seem very important to him. George's dad is from Dublin originally, and he has a huge family living there still. They love coming 'over the water' as George's dad puts it, and they all come together, which must be a bit intimidating for the other people on the ferry. With all the husbands, wives and children they count up to about thirty people. They literally take over the bed and breakfast hotel near George's house.

George's mum came from Jamaica when she was fifteen, and still has such a broad accent that I find her a bit hard to understand sometimes. But her sister and family are even worse! Then she has both her parents here in England (they live just round the corner to her) and a tribe of cousins and people she calls 'aunty' and 'uncle' who don't really seem to be relatives but who come over for family reunions just the same. There are even more aunties in Spain and in Malta – even they came, with their families.

As usual, George's dad booked the local church hall and with all the family there it was about eighty people! George seemed to know each and every one of them, and chatted all night. The spooky thing was, they knew all about me, too. People I have never clapped eyes on before in my life were asking me how Lizzie was doing, and how I was enjoying the 'A' levels, and whether my mum was going back to work yet – one of the mysterious Jamaican aunties even asked if I had lost weight, as I looked much more scrawny than my photo. So they knew all about me, and I knew nothing at all about them. I told George it was like being in a horror movie or something, but he just laughed and said, 'Yeah, I know. Aren't they great?' He is so proud of his family. He doesn't see that for someone not brought up to it a huge

4

family is a bit overwhelming. Later I found out that George's mum writes to half a dozen of them every week, and the letters get shared around. She seems to have told them an awful lot about George and me, and not all of it strictly truthful. For instance, I do have strong feelings for George but as far as I know we haven't planned to marry, and certainly haven't planned to marry on a beach in Jamaica, as his Aunty Jessica seemed to think.

It was fun, but absolutely exhausting. I just don't know how George kept going – he looked like the evening had only just started when I said I had to go home and go to bed. Thank God for my small, ordinary family. I can keep track of their names, I only have to repeat the same news a couple of times to get it right through the family, and I don't have to start saving for their Christmas presents in January. And now to sleep – I just can't keep my eyes open, and my head is swimming with images of strange faces and huge smiles.

October 13th

Jenny went to a family party at George's last night. She has met his parents before, of course, and others in the family at his sister's wedding, but this was the first time she had been invited to meet the whole extended family, which I hear is quite a tribe. Jenny came home a bit earlier than expected, claiming she was tired. She looked shell-shocked, not just tired. When I asked what she had thought of George's family (meaning, of course, that what I really wanted to know was what they thought of her) she only said, 'Mum, there are so MANY of them' and trailed upstairs to bed. I was left on tenterhooks until the morning. Then Jenny told me that half the world is related to George in some way or other. As she describes it, it doesn't sound like much of an

5

exaggeration, either. Poor girl — I gather George's family is very close-knit on both sides, and Alicia (George's mum) is a phenomenal letter writer, so all the rellies knew about Jenny even though she didn't know about them.

It must be fun to have such a large family. I expect Jenny would love to have a huge hoard of relatives around her, taking an interest and giving her centre stage. Our little family must appear very dull by comparison.

October 22nd

George and I have hardly seen each other all week. For a start, Mum and Dad have insisted that I spend more time studying, and so they have banned me from going out on school nights, except for Wednesdays when I go babysitting. So that means we can only get together on Friday, Saturday and Sunday. George has just started a new practical block on the geriatrics ward, so on Saturday and Sunday he was either working or tired out. I tried to be understanding, but I feel like my life is turning into the life of one of those sad people who live for work and nothing else. What do Mum and Dad want, exactly? A normal person who hopes to get 'A' levels with reasonable grades should surely be enough. They seem to be aiming for an egghead weirdo professor who nobody wants to spend time with. I wish Mum would get a life of her own, and stop worrying about mine.

Mum is agonising over whether to go back to work or not. She says she'll feel guilty if she leaves Lizzie with a childminder, because she never did that with Jon and me. But if she doesn't go back she'll feel guilty about not 'reaching her potential', whatever that means (she has these throwbacks to her Sixties youth, sometimes, when everyone seemed to be on a journey to discover themselves but no-one ever arrived. Sad).

6

Jon and I think she should go back. While she's been at home she's had much more time to interfere with our lives. Poor old Jon has had his lego models dismantled and his carefully hoarded craft kits (sweet wrappers and cereal boxes to you and me) thrown out so many times he's lost count. Mum gets this guilt thing about lounging around at home doing nothing except watching Lizzie and drinking coffee with her friends, so every now and then she has a mega-purge on the bedrooms and roots out every last speck. I manage to fight her off mine by cleaning it myself (not that it stops her nagging at me to do it far more often than it needs doing) but Jon's seven-years-old cleaning style isn't up to scratch, so Mum does it herself.

I would usually be looking forward to a half-term break round about this time of year, and planning some really good things to do. But although half-term is actually next week, there's no point in planning anything and I may as well be at school. George is working, Mum will be at home all day and when I'm not slogging my way through a mountain of Biology and History coursework I'll be trying to catch up on the reading I'm supposed to be doing for English or babysitting for Mum. Some break, huh?

24th October

I do feel I ought to let my department know soon whether or not I'll be coming back to work. The woman who took my place is quite keen to stay on, apparently, but will need to look for a new job in good time if I go back. I know the children will be quite keen to have me at home; we certainly spend more time together and lead more organized lives these days, in spite of having a baby around. But I think I just don't have it in me to go through all that mumsy stuff again.

7

Lizzie is quite an easy-going baby, but it's still very hard work. She has that uncanny knack many babies have of sensing when I'm about to put my feet up for a snatched coffee break, and waking up for a feed. Just lately she seems to be quite miserable a lot of the time. However hard I work at getting a household routine established, I never seem to make any progress. The house seems far messier now than it ever did when I was out at work. Maybe I didn't notice because there was too much to do, but it seems like I can never have all the rooms in the house clean and tidy at the same time. I used not to take much notice of housework, as long as the kitchen and bathrooms were clean: now I seem to run all over the house, and the state of the bedrooms really gets on my nerves. So on top of all the usual domestic stuff and the extra work a baby creates, I have to clean through everywhere. I feel like a cleaning and milk machine. It doesn't help when Jenny comes home to find me having a cup of tea with another harrassed mum looking for support and raises her eyebrows before telling me what a hard day she's had, as if I've done nothing but sit around.

I am turning into a moaning Minnie, and everyone is getting on my nerves. Everyone. Mike is wrapped up in his work and doesn't seem to notice; Lizzie sees me as an unstoppable machine provided from on high to slave to her every whim; Jon rewards me for cleaning up after him by throwing tantrums about grotty bits of paper that I throw away; Jenny treats me like a jailor just because I'm insisting that she concentrates on schoolwork on weeknights and sees George at weekends. I told her she would be grateful to me one day, when she gets good 'A' level results. She said, 'Mother, get a life'.

I am the only person who feels sorry for me. Perhaps I should go back to work, before I end up as a depression statistic. Trouble is, with every day it's *harder and harder to get out of bed, never mind holding down a job and running a house and family. I wish I could just curl up and go to sleep, and wake up in ten years or so.*

October 27th

Mum wouldn't get out of bed today. She said she ached all over, and just couldn't face it. She looked terrible – white, with dark grey bits around her eyes. Dad said he would stay home, but since I was on half term I decided to rise to the challenge and take charge myself. At least it would make a change from coursework, and George loves all that family sticking together stuff. I telephoned him to see if he would mind coming over to our house instead of going out (Mum having relaxed her idiotic rule about not seeing each other, at least over half-term). He said that would be fine, and I could tell he was impressed by my concern about my little brother and sister.

I decided to set a good example to Mum and show her how much could be achieved with a little organization. I made a list of targets for the day:

clean every room (except Mum and Dad's room)

tidy up the garden shed

take Jon and Lizzie to the park

do the ironing (Mum lets it mount up quite unnecessarily)

cook dinner

bake a cake

Unfortunately the day didn't pan out quite as I had planned. The telephone kept ringing, usually just as I was changing Lizzie's nappy or half-way up the stairs with a drink for Mum or on the other side of the house hoovering. Someone came to service the boiler, and so the kitchen was out of action for the very timeslot I had set aside for the baking of a cake. Lizzie sleeps almost all day when she's with Mum, but today she just grizzled whenever she woke up and I had to lug her around with me whatever I was doing, so in the end I had to forget the hoovering and just do a bit of dusting instead. Mum still breast-feeds Lizzie, so I had to keep running up and down the stairs delivering her to Mum, collecting her to put in her pram, bribing Jon to rock her to sleep, changing nappies (which she promptly filled immediately, almost every time!).

I sorted the laundry but didn't actually get a chance to load anything into the machine before Jon was whingeing about wanting his lunch. After I had cooked fish fingers and noodles and washed up I was too tired to contemplate the park, but I had promised Jon so he dragged me out anyway. It took nearly half an hour to get Lizzie ready, by the time I'd changed her nappy, found her coat and bonnet and bootees, got the pram ready etc. etc. etc. – and then Jon announced that he couldn't find his shoes. After we found them, Lizzie was getting grizzly and had to be cuddled off to sleep.

Finally we all got out of the front door. By the time we'd been in the park ten minutes, Lizzie woke up and started to get hungry. Not a lot I could do about that, with a breast-fed baby. I tried to soothe her out of it, but she wouldn't be bought off, so when her wails reached screaming pitch we had to come home, with Jon moaning it wasn't fair and he hadn't wanted a baby sister anyway, and me wondering what on earth we could eat for dinner, as I had forgotten to bring any money for the shops.

I gave Jon fish fingers and noodles again for tea, and he didn't mind. Mum had some toast and egg, and didn't look interested in hearing the day's news. She lay down again and closed her eyes. Dad saved the day by coming home early for once and bringing a Chinese takeaway with him. All in all, it wasn't too bad. I hope Mum is better tomorrow.

Mum isn't any better. I took Lizzie in to her and she started to cry, and told me to take her away. Well I couldn't, because she needed feeding, so I just sort of stood there with Lizzie getting more and more frantic, waiting for Mum to do something. She just lay there, crying. Then Jon came in, and he started crying too. Just as well Dad came out of the bathroom when he did, or we would all have been at it. Dad told me to take Jon down and give him some breakfast, and he took Lizzie and sat by Mum. A couple of minutes later Lizzie stopped crying in that very sudden way that means her mouth has been plugged. So Mum must have decided to feed her after all.

I was so worried that I couldn't concentrate on anything, and Jon ate his way through three pieces of burnt toast without a murmur. Finally Dad came down and said he was going to call the doctor, and could I cope for another day if he came back as early as he could? Of course I said yes, but I didn't know how I was going to manage. I mean, I've read about these women who get post-natal depression and they have to be constantly watched, and they can't look after their babies for months. I love Lizzie to pieces, but I'm not sure I can sacrifice my whole life for her. Dad said he thought Mum was just overtired, but he wanted the doctor to make sure she was O.K. I think Dad's just as worried as me, but he doesn't want to show it. Anyway, he went off to the office to try and organize the next few days so that he can work at home, and I was left trying to explain to Jon why our mother cries whenever you look at her.

I went up to get Lizzie after a while and she and Mum were both asleep. Lizzie was sort of hanging on to Mum's nipple, and I gently unwedged her and put Mum's nightie back together without Mum even opening an eye. I put Lizzie down in the pram and set to work on all the stuff I tried to get done yesterday. I didn't have

11

much more luck than I did then. I suppose all this is a lot easier for Mum, since she doesn't have a life and she's much more used to domestic routine. All the same, it did make me think. There's a lot more to running a house and looking after a baby than I realized. I think I won't have children until I can afford a nanny. And a housekeeper.

Thank God for my lovely, lovely George, who had a day off today. He phoned to see how Mum was, and when I told him he came right over and took charge. He went up to see Mum and then he came down and took a tin of baby milk, a bottle and a pack of steriliser tablets out of his coat pockets. He said he'd stopped at the chemist, just in case Mum wasn't well enough to feed Lizzie. She'd agreed to let him try Lizzie on baby milk. How many men of his age would come up with that? I was so proud of him, but he just shrugged and said when you had as many brothers and sisters as he has, you've seen it all. By the time Dad arrived back at lunchtime, the house had been cleaned, Jon was happily engrossed in a video, George was stirring some soup and Lizzie was lying in her pram gurgling up at the ceiling and looking well content.

Mum slept almost all day, until the doctor came about three o'clock. She says Mum hasn't got post-natal depression exactly, but she is worn out and seems to have a viral infection as well. The doc. reckons the milk Mum is producing at the moment isn't enough for Lizzie and Mum and she have decided it's best to give up breast-feeding her. Poor old Mum – she went on and on while she was pregnant about how important it is to feed a baby yourself, but I suppose a few weeks is at least a good start.

George and I went to the pub for a quiet drink once Jon was in bed. Mum looked a bit better when I took him in to say goodnight. She's got to stay in bed at least another couple of days, but Dad's going to be home most of the time so we should be all right.

Famous last words. Dad went down with the same virus as Mum the very next day, so I had two of them to look after, as well as Lizzie and Jon. I don't think Dad feels as bad as Mum, but I have noticed that when a man goes down with something it's like multiplying the effect on a woman by ten. George says that's really sexist. He also admits it's probably true. If it hadn't been for my friends, I just don't know how I would have survived. Sadie, Cathy and George all rallied round and helped out with the kids while I did the housework. George's mum sent round a huge Jamaican chicken casserole and a mountain of rice and peas. We all lived off that and bread and butter – it was a lovely casserole, but it did get a bit boring by the third day.

Dad is fine today, and Mum got up for the first time since she felt poorly. She still looks white and washed out. I told her I thought that was very fitting, this being Hallowe'en. If anyone comes trick or treating, I think she should answer the door – I don't think we'll have any trouble.

Lizzie is much more cheery now that she is on baby milk. Mum must find that awful, that her milk wasn't good enough. It's not her fault she was ill, but maybe she is a bit old for all this anyway.

George came round to help with cooking dinner. I had promised Jon and his best friend a Hallowe'en feast, and they dressed up in spiderman suits and horrible masks for the occasion. We made them meatballs (we called them sheep's eyes) with spaghetti (mortals' intestines) and broccoli smothered in ketchup (witches' lungs). We put red food colouring in lemonade to make Bloody Drink, and black jelly for dessert. Jon thought it was all great, and drove us mad with jokes about where was his bloody drink, pass him his bloody drink, ho ho. Still, he was quite cute. And while I got him ready for bed and read him a gentle, witchy story, George did all the washing up. Mum and Dad both told him they thought he was great, and thanked him for helping out. George gave one of those gorgeous smiles, and said it had all made him realize how much he wants a family of his own. I didn't say anything!

November 2nd

At last I feel more like myself again. I truly thought I was sinking into a pit these last couple of weeks, but it turns out it was nothing more dramatic than a flu-type virus plus a touch of post-baby blues and more than a touch of exhaustion. Dr Carter says I'm really suffering from what she calls Superwoman virus, quite common in the older mother apparently. You run yourself ragged trying to prove how well you can do everything, and how having a baby hasn't made the least bit of difference: you end up feeling like an old hag. She hit the nail on the head exactly. I have been trying to do far more than I ever did even before Lizzie was born. I am going to try and drop my standards and hang loose a bit more. I'm not going back to work, either. Mike says that unless I desperately want to, there's no point. We don't need the money, and he'd rather see me doing some of the things I'd always talked about doing. It's true there were all sorts of classes and hobbies I wanted to start when I was at home with Jenny and then with Jon. In those days we didn't have the money, and then when I went back to work and Mike got promoted I had the money, but I didn't have the time. Now I'm going to spend a bit of time by myself, for myself. Mike has even got the telephone number of his secretary's childminder, who is happy to have Lizzie for a few hours when I feel like a break. I thought he didn't care, but all this time he's been worrying and trying to work out what to do. I do love him.

14

*Talking about love, Jenny and George positively
shine with it. I looked at them today, playing with
Lizzie and talking about some CD they've bought
together, and I could just see them in twenty years
time, still together and chatting away. George told us
a couple of days ago that he plans to have lots of
children. He certainly copes very well with Lizzie and
Jon, and I think he'll make a good husband and
father. Not that I want Jenny to meet Mr Right just
yet – George is only her second steady boyfriend and
I hope she'll have a few more chances before she
settles down. Still, she could do worse than someone
like him.*

November 4th

My little brother has gone up in my estimation. He has
always been such a little goody two-shoes, or so I
thought. But today, one of our neighbours came to tell
Mum that she had seen him asking people for money
outside the local newsagents. He and another little boy
had a raggedy old guy in a pram, she said, and were
'begging for money from passers by'. Now a sensible
person would call it 'penny for the guy-ing' and it would
be no big deal, but we were dealing with Mrs Smart from
Number 42. She implied Mum had no idea what her
children were doing, or cared very much either. Mum
kept her cool remarkably well and wouldn't be drawn
into a fight, but I could see she was shaken. She thanked
Mrs Smart for letting her know, and said she would deal
with it. You could see Mrs Smart wanted to make more
of a meal of it, but she had no luck – all those years of
dealing with people in Casualty reception seem to have
paid off for Mum. Personally, I would have smacked her
one, the trouble-making old bag.

Mrs Smart has been looking for trouble ever since she
accosted George and me about our perfectly natural

15

wish to kiss each other goodnight when he walks me home. She came out to tell us that we were lowering the tone of the neighbourhood, 'gnawing away at each other like a couple of animals who haven't been fed for days' as she put it. George said he would be more careful now that he knew there were peeping toms in the neighbourhood! Her face was a picture – she spluttered a bit, and then bustled back indoors like an angry little insect that missed its dinner. I think it's fair to say she took an instant dislike to George then and there, and she's never been particularly fond of me.

Anyway, back to Jon. He had told Mum he was going to be at Carlo's house – Carlo is his best friend, and looks as though butter wouldn't melt in his mouth. Jon's been going there quite a lot lately, but Mum thought it was because of the baby, and her not being well and so on. Carlo's an only child, and his mum lets them run wild and make all the noise they want. But apparently they hatched this little scheme while they were having their hallowe'en dinner at our place last week. Both the families had said they could have some sparklers at home and then go to an organized display. But they wanted their very own fireworks party. So they made a guy and they've been out together lots of times to get money. Carlo's mum thought he was at our house.

They managed to raise twelve pounds, and they've already bought a box of fireworks. I think that's very enterprising of them. It's not as if they went a long way from home. But Mum and Dad hit the roof. They have spoken to Carlo's parents on the telephone, and the two boys are not allowed to play together for a week. Also, Dad has taken the fireworks away and both little boys have been told they won't be having fireworks at all. I think that's really mean and over the top, and I told Mum so. She told me to stay out of it! She wasn't even prepared to listen (I think she's still a bit unbalanced from being ill, maybe).

So, Jon has sobbed himself to sleep, Mum is raging

downstairs on the sofa, claiming that Jon is going to turn into some kind of delinquent and what can she do to get through to him' etc. etc. Dad is saying nothing, just looking grim and passing Mum the hankies. What a fuss. They should be grateful Jon has a bit of gumph.

4th November

Our neighbour Mrs Smart came to see me today. She has always been rather nosy and interfering, but I try not to take any notice. Today I could see by the light in her eye and the sense of wild anticipation as she hurried across the road to our house that she had some dirt to dish. I was taken by surprise, unloading the shopping from the car; before I knew it she was somehow in my kitchen, sipping a cup of tea and telling me that Jon and Carlo have been going out with their guy regularly since the half-term holiday, collecting money for fireworks. She only saw them herself yesterday, but other neighbours have told her that wasn't the first time. I could just imagine the little gossip circle wondering whom they should send. Mrs Smart was, of course, the obvious choice. No-one wanted to bring bad tidings, but she felt it was her duty as someone who had once had small children herself... etc.

It was so humiliating. She asked if I was coping with all the children (that little stress on the word ALL that in itself seems to imply I have no self-control and have children by the hundred) and assured me that if ever I needed help all I had to do was ask (in other words, I'm not up to the job).

Her children are long grown, of course, and if ever they put a foot out of line she has obviously forgotten it. Her son is a dentist in Holland, and her daughter married a company executive and moved to America. I'm sure they chose foreign countries to get away from her: I know I would.

All the same, it's a shock to know that Jon is prepared to lie to us, never mind all the rest of it. At first he denied it when I tackled him, claiming he really was at Carlo's and it must have been someone else Mrs Smart saw. Then I said I would call Carlo's mum and check, and he started crying. He and Carlo had decided to have their own fireworks night, and they knew we wouldn't let them have fireworks so they couldn't ask for the money.

He made it all sound so simple and logical. How could I explain to him why it was so wrong? I can't bear to think of what kind of people those two little boys might have ended up being involved with. What if someone had tried to persuade them to go with him? Or tricked them into accepting money for 'favours'? Or simply abducted them off the street? And what if they had gone off to some piece of wasteground far away from adults' eyes to let off their fireworks? What if one of them had been injured or killed? Jon does not seem to have any idea about the risks he took. Nor has Carlo, according to his family. Lucia is as shocked as we are. She has told Carlo he must stay away from Jon for a week, and only when he shows he understands what he has done wrong will he be allowed out to play at all. She also asked us to destroy the fireworks, which Jon handed over straight away once he knew they had been caught out. Obviously we can't let them have the fireworks, because that would be rewarding them for doing wrong, but I'm at a loss to know what to do with them. Perhaps George will take them for his little sisters, if Alicia won't be offended.

Poor Jon. He has been very naughty, but I can't help feeling sorry for him. He's only just beginning to realize how serious it all was: us not knowing where he was, the begging, the dishonesty, the risks of letting off fireworks alone, and I suspect most of all the knowledge that Dad and I won't find it easy to trust him now. It all seems like punishment enough, but Mike has insisted that there will be no firework display for him tomorrow.

Jenny thinks we are over-reacting and has made it all far worse by saying so in front of Jon. She claims I am going over the top because Mrs Smart got involved and I'm trying to prove something to her. I think she hit just a bit too close to home. At the time I was so mad I could have strangled her, but now I've calmed down a bit I wish we had not been quite as hard on our little son as we were. It's too late now, though. Tomorrow, when everyone else is watching the sky light up and dancing round the bonfire, we will be at home listening to the noises and trying not to look at each other.

November 6th

Bonfire night was not a happy event in our family history. I hope we can all laugh about it in years to come, but at the moment we're trying to forget it. Jon's reproachful face whenever he heard a rocket going up from someone's garden, and his solitary figure at the window watching to see signs of other people's fireworks almost broke my heart. Mike actually relented somewhat and brought home some sparklers. Jon brightened a little bit, but it didn't save the general tone of the evening, which was awful.

George had taken the fireworks away quite happily, but he and Jenny were brewing for a fight. George could fully understand why we were so upset about what Jon did, but Jenny said it was nothing to keep going on about. I could tell by the looks on their faces that there was going to be one almighty row over it after they'd left. Sure enough, Jenny came back alone at about eight o'clock with a face like thunder, and said would it be all right if she took Jon out for a little while before he went to bed, so he could see the bonfires in other people's gardens and watch some fireworks that way? She said it would really sink in to him what he had thrown away by being so naughty, and next year he would know better. I took all that to mean she and George had fought over whether our approach to Jon was right or not, and Jenny had lost. I also had a very strong feeling that Jenny was planning to do more than simply walk around with Jon looking over other people's fences. She was no doubt planning some kind of treat, probably to do with fireworks at a friend's house. I let it go without challenging her, though. She's old enough to be responsible, and in truth I do believe Jon has suffered enough. So I pretended I believed what she was saying. When they came back, she had obviously told Jon not to look as if he had had a good time. His expression was bizarre. He was trying to look sad, like a kid who has missed out on fireworks, but he just looked twitchy. I pretended not to notice. The sooner we put this sad and sorry episode behind us, the better.

Jenny has been sitting all evening trying to look like someone who is definitely NOT waiting for a telephone call. George called her at about ten last night and I could hear Jenny's raised voice through the door. She went to bed with a bare 'goodnight' and was not at all communicative at breakfast either. I must admit I was too busy with Jon and Lizzie to pay much attention to her, but I hope she and George are O.K.

6th November

George and I had a row last night, and I don't even know what it was all about, not really. It started with him taking

20

Mum's side over this ridiculous thing with Jon. I suggested we smuggle him out round to George's and let him join in there, since after all he had contributed to the fireworks. George said it just showed how daft I could be, and how could I even think about undoing the lesson my parents were trying to teach Jon? He gave me this long lecture about how he had seen all the things that can happen to children. Fair enough, I hadn't really thought through how risky it was for Jon and Carlo to plan what they did, but there was no need to make me feel stupid.

Anyway, somehow we moved off the point about fireworks and on to George not giving me enough time. He seems to belong to everybody – wherever we go people seem to know him or, even worse, he gets talking to a complete stranger and they end up chatting for ages. I know this should make me proud – his easy going charm is one of the things I loved him for, right from the very first. But does he have to be charming to *everybody*, all the time? George said I was being possessive, and that was not something he found attractive in a woman. Then I called him a sexist pig, he called me self-centred, I said he was already like an old man and he said that was better than staying a child for ever...it all went on from there, and it was horrible. I stormed out, and came back home for Jon. I took him straight off to the shops (not the ones Mrs Smart spies over, of course) and then I took him over to the park and we had our own private firework display. His little face lit up when he realized what we were doing. I told him that he must never tell Mum and Dad or they'd do their pieces, and I made sure he practised a disappointed look for when we got home. Nice touch, that. Mum was completely fooled. She had calmed down quite a bit, and was very tender and loving. Jon not only got his fireworks, but he got to stay up later than usual AND still have a bedtime story. I don't suppose George would approve, but what do I care? He can rot in his own smug, self-righteous, pompous stew for all I care.

He didn't phone me tonight. But I'm not going to go crawling to him. I'm just going to wait until he sees how wrong he's been, and then I'm going to be very gracious and forgiving. If only he phones.

9th November

There has been a cloud hanging over us all since Jon's penny for the guy escapade. He has been a mutinous little boy, saying childish and spiteful things to Lizzie (who, of course, doesn't understand, and smiles at him) and he and Carlo are no longer friends. Miss Treetop mentioned this to me when I went to pick Jon up from school: she said each seems to blame the other for them getting into trouble, and they are both becoming quite a disruptive element in the class. She seems to think it will be a passing phase, but I'm beginning to wonder if we shouldn't have handled the thing differently.

Jenny and George also had a major row that night, and neither one of them seems prepared to call the other to make it up. How well I remember those days: the burning indignation and pride, the determination not to be the one to say sorry, and the awful hurt and misery of realizing that the other person isn't going to make the first move either. As I got older I began to understand that life is simply too short to waste time worrying about who is at fault when you have an argument: the important thing is to talk it through and move on, not fester over it. But there's no point in telling Jenny that. She has to learn it for herself, and follow the same sorry, suffering path that her mother did. In the meantime, living with her is like living with a ticking time bomb. She is constantly snappy, and you never know when the next major explosion will be. The joys of motherhood? Just don't ask me to count them.

George was waiting for me at the gate when I left college today. His expression was so sweet that although he didn't say anything I forgave him on the spot. I still think he was wrong to say what he did, but the important thing is, I love him. I wonder if he feels the same way about me? Does he think *I* was wrong, but he loves me and so will overlook it? Well, who cares? We are back together again, and that's all that really counts.

Sadie and Adam came into the youth centre just as George and I were getting down to some serious making up tonight, and they both laughed and said how glad they were that we were back together. They seem like an old married couple, those two. They never argue in any serious way, and they don't do anything unless it's together. Not like Cathy and Ted, who are still painting the town red a couple of nights a week and living completely separate lives the rest of the time. He goes back to his wife and family, and she sees nothing wrong in having a couple of lads on standby when he's not available (but she hasn't told him).

George and I were talking about that tonight, and about how unsatisfying a relationship like that must be. How can you ever trust someone to tell you the truth about anything, once you know they are prepared to lie about such a big thing? George says Cathy's been brought up on deceit and lies, with her mother being such a heavy drinker, so it seems O.K. to her. But I would have thought that seeing her mum slowly disintegrating and constantly catching her out in all sorts of lies would have made Cathy even more determined to be open and honest.

Anyway, we got talking about honesty, and we both promised that we would always be totally open and honest with each other, even if that was difficult or painful. That's when George told me he's always had a bit of a fancy for Louise Ann Maynard! She's in my

23

English group, and comes to youth club sometimes. George says she's got a fantastic figure and huge, beautiful, brown eyes. He was smiling as he said it and I could see he was trying to wind me up, so I laughed and said if he liked women who looked like cows, what was he doing with me? He gave me a long, lovely kiss and said he could never really look at anyone else.

All the same, I'd better pay a bit more attention to Louise Ann Maynard. If she tries to get her claws into my man, she'll have a fight on her hands.

15th November

It's all on again with Jenny and George, thank goodness. That tight-lipped don't-care expression of hers was beginning to get to me. I don't know who broke the ice first. Jenny just announced, with very elaborate casualness, that she would be going out with George and might be back late. I'm happy to see them back together; they're a nice, safe match for each other (though I would never dream of saying such a thing to Jenny, of course!).

Jon is a lot more cheerful now, too, and he and Carlo are friends again. They are making their own Christmas decorations to sell and make some money for presents. Heaven help us, we have already had to buy some of them: sad-looking lumps of sticky paper and sparkly ribbon. They're not even made with loving care so that you can be sentimentally proud; they're churned out in a little man's business enterprise way. Carlo even offered me a 'three for the price of two' deal yesterday! I hope they lose enthusiasm soon – then I can quietly dispose of their wares before the question arises of where we are going to hang them!

George and I sat down to plan our Christmas list today. It is strange, making a joint list. I have never done it before, but it feels good to think that presents will come from both of us, not just one. We are like one person. It's cheaper, too.

The brat, Jon, offered to sell us some of his 'hand-crafted, esscloosive' tree decorations. He and Carlo (of course, who else?) have gone into business again. The decorations are disgustingly ugly, and it isn't wise to touch them as they are basically scrunched-up balls of paper with tatty bits of ribbon glued on at a ratio of about one ton of glue per bow. Once you have one in your hand it tends to stay there – which could, I suppose, be a clever marketing ploy to make you feel obliged to buy one. I have told Jon exactly where to stick his 'esscloosive creations' but Mum is a real sucker. She thinks they're cute, and she's bought at least half a dozen. I can see our living room on Christmas Eve now – walls festooned with hand-made newspaper streamers, the tree dripping glue and cheap ribbon, and fat cat Jon counting up his profits before revealing the presents he has bought for all us – a set of Christmas decorations each, no doubt.

Louise Ann Maynard was down at the club today. She came over to sit with us, and asked me about the essay we have to do for the end of term. I dealt with it as quickly as I could, but then George asked her something and soon they were chatting away and she was sort of cemented in for the evening. It's not that I'm jealous or anything, but she is a known man eater and George is a bit of an innocent when it comes to women. He always assumes that what you see is what you get. He doesn't understand that when you say one thing you sometimes mean something completely different, and he can't read around what's *not* said, only what *is*. I try to explain the more devious workings of people's minds, but he just laughs and says I ought to go in for one of those television psychology jobs. He doesn't have a devious bone in his body. Letting Louise Ann Maynard come anywhere near him is like serving him ready-cooked on a platter and inviting her to try a piece.

When he went to the loo, Louise Ann Maynard told me she thought George was gorgeous, and that I was very lucky. I decided not to tell George about that.

2nd December 1995

George and I went Christmas shopping yesterday. We spent all day buying little bits and pieces – we got some lovely things for his sisters. George's family are very easy to buy for – the little ones love paint and paper-type things and the older ones are content to drown in Body Shop bubbles. George only has one brother, and he is in to big band music. I had to send George in alone to get 'The Best of James Last and his Orchestra' tape we bought for him. I would have died if my friends had seen me with it. For Grace (George's just-married sister) we bought some rather elegant tree decorations for their first ever tree. Afterwards, Jon insisted on seeing everything we'd bought, and when he saw the decorations he was genuinely surprised that we hadn't gone to him instead. He could apparently have made the same thing at a fraction of the price. What will that child come to? I can just picture him at his market stall, a graduate of the Wide Boy Sales Academy.

We still have to get presents for George's parents, Mum and Dad, and Jon, but we ran out of steam and money. Dad is going to pay me to do some of his routine paperwork at the weekend, so that'll be a help. I have several babysitting jobs looming as well, as people go off to their office and family parties and all the rest of it. Christmas is a curious season – you'd think old people would try and spread their fun over the year, but everyone seems to cram parties into two or three weeks, and then go back to boring routine for another whole year. Dad reckons that if he goes to all his official functions, he'll have eaten eleven Christmas dinners before the day itself!

Mum is getting a bit frazzled. The grandparents (all four of them) are coming two days after Christmas, so it will all be happening twice in our house. We are having a quiet day together on the 25th, for Lizzie's first Christmas, and a big family day on the 28th. I suspect Mum will use the 25th as a practice run for some of the things she wants to cook to impress the grands. There are little notes everywhere – lists, timetables, recipe ideas. She has bought all the Christmas versions of the women's magazines and cuts out the recipes she wants to have a go at. (I have quietly chucked away the carrot and coriander bake in orange juice – sounds gross). She's going to end up in a complete mess – I've seen the signs before.

I am doing my best to be helpful, but until school finishes there's not a lot I can do. It doesn't look as if my teachers (especially the American lunatic) know that Christmas is coming – they simply see the break as an opportunity to catch up on background reading and work on an extra essay or two. I don't think they have a life at all.

3rd December

I have laid down my battle plans for Christmas with almost military precision this year. With a little baby to care for and the whole family arriving before New Year, it's the only way to survive. I feel very calm and in control. It's actually quite creative, planning ahead and making lists. I've noted everything down in my diary – when to do the cards, when to pick up the turkey etc. Since we are going to be celebrating

Christmas twice, I want to try out a few new ideas rather than cook the same thing over again. There are some lovely vegetarian alternatives to the traditional fare, and I plan to have a go at them. Most years I'm running around like a headless chicken throughout December, racing against time to get everything done and get to work as well. Now that I'm not at work, it seems like a breeze.

Jenny and George have been a big help. I wonder if all the children in George's family are as helpful and respectful as he is, or did he just drop straight from heaven? He'll make a wonderful nurse. My only concern about him and Jenny is that he is perhaps too willing to let her boss him about. It's great to be easygoing, but I wish he had just a bit of a temper. She needs not to get away with things sometimes.

Jon has given up making decorations at last. He and Carlo raised four pounds each (they both have indulgent families) and Jon got extra pocket money for his feeble attempts to wash the car as well. Mike is taking Jon out to get his Christmas shopping next week. I told him not to bother to spend his hard-earned money on Lizzie, who won't understand the concept of a gift, or be able to unwrap anything. He looked at me as though I was planning to serve up his baby sister as a side vegetable. How could I think of leaving her out? He then grilled me over whether Mike and I were going to buy a present for her, and whether we had left him out on his first Christmas. He was outraged. I reassured him that Lizzie would be getting a present from us (I didn't tell him that apart from a small teddy it was all useful stuff like clothes and a nappy changing table that we would have bought anyway).

Only one more week of school – I can hardly wait. The 'A' level teachers have all agreed that work will continue as normal right up to the last day, because they're worried about losing the time and meeting the syllabus requirements. That's what they say. The truth is probably that they can't stand the thought of us slowing down a bit or even – gasp, shock horror! – having FUN.

We've been reading 'Much Ado About Nothing' this week. It's not one of our texts but Jack J. Jackson calls it 'light relief from the more tragic elements of our Shakespearian load'. No kidding. Anyway, I love that part when Beatrix tells Hero (who is a girl, though she has a bloke's name) to have a snog with her man. She doesn't say snog, of course, this being the great Bard. She says 'stop his mouth with a kiss'. It's so romantic, that.

I have stopped George's mouth with many kisses lately. That's partly because he has one of the most kissable mouths to stop in the whole country, but also to remind him that I'm not such a bad kisser myself. Louise Ann Maynard has joined the little group of sad people who are organising the Christmas disco at the youth centre. Frankly, George and I feel a bit old for all that now, and we don't go to the centre very much. But Louise Ann Maynard has somehow managed to persuade George to help out with the arrangements. He's working really hard for his nursing assessment, and I told him not to be an idiot and overload himself. But he's really in to all that community spirit stuff, and he has loads of ideas for decorating the hall, getting the teenyboppers along and so on. George never really listens to my point of view – he pretends to, but then he goes his own sweet way. You either give in, or get left behind.

In the end, I had a choice. I could leave him to it – and to Louise Ann – or I could join in too. So I underwent a magical conversion and showed some enthusiasm myself. Now George has told Maneater Maynard that I'm on the committee too. It will be worth all the tedious running around just to know that her plans to get my man are being thwarted at every turn.

Jack J. Jackson has volunteered to come along and be the bouncer for the evening. For some reason, he managed to be appointed the school-youth centre link person. Presumably our illustrious head, who is so far gone that even a brain transplant would offer only limited hope, agrees with Jack J. that he's a real cool dude who has a feel for where it's at with the young people, know whaddi mean? On reflection, he's a good choice. One look at him doing his cool tough-guy act in his suede boots, and people will fall about laughing; they'll have no energy to cause trouble.

15th December

I can hardly believe the transformation in Jenny since she and George got together. He seems to have been a positive influence on her right from the start. She has even got stuck in to arranging the local youth centre entertainment. She would never have done that in the past. She would have turned up her nose and said how naff it was to sit on committees planning lives for people who don't have one. She would not have been seen dead at a youth club party, still less throw in her lot with those who sought to organize one. Yet here she is, dutifully writing down 'things to do' and discussing with George the merits of soft or flashing lights etc etc. Mike smiled wryly when I told him and said that, knowing Jenny, there's some devious little plan involved, but I'm not so sure. After all, we have tried to bring her up to think of others, and with some idea of the value of serving the community. It all seems to have come to fruition, especially since she has taken up with a boy who shares those ideals.

It seems impossible that it will be Christmas in only ten days, I haven't finished half the things I planned to do. But I'm not going to get upset about it, just let it all flow. Mike suggested we could even try and book a table somewhere for the grandparents' visit. I've never considered it before, but I'm tempted. It will not be an enjoyable time for any of us if I'm in such a frazzle that everyone is made to rush around feeling miserable. As long as the children have their presents and there is food in the house, we'll be fine. So I've thrown away the lists and the schedules, and it was a truly liberating experience. Christmas will be a peaceful, relaxing time with no pressures. If the turkey goes wrong, we'll eat egg and chips instead. What does it matter?

17th December

Mum has finally fallen off her trolley. I could see it coming, with all the stress and the rushing around, and looking after a baby and being too old to cope with that sort of thing. She came into the kitchen a couple of nights ago and threw away all her carefully planned lists and menus. She told us that Christmas was not supposed to be about all this, and we would have a happier time 'going with the flow'. We all breathed a sigh of relief at first. Usually round about this time Mum starts dishing out the orders and every spare moment is spent cleaning, polishing, running to the shops for some forgotten ingredient or being the kichen assistant while she cooks and crams the freezer with food that no-one's allowed to eat.

After a moment, realization dawned. Mum's version of letting it all flow means NO cooking ahead, NO exotic dishes, and possibly NO TURKEY. She has ordered two, one for the 25th and one for the 28th, but now she says they can always be frozen for another time, and pork chops will be easier. Is this a wind-up, or what? George is coming round for Christmas Day, because his family are going up to some aunty's or other. Their family celebration is going to be on Boxing Day, and they've invited me. How am I going to feel, when I arrive at his house to be greeted with a mound of traditional food and carefully planned entertainment, knowing that we fed him a pork chop and oven chips because my mum discovered the true meaning of Christmas? I tried to reason with her, but she's so far off her trolley there was no point. I asked Dad to help, but he just shrugged and said since all the arrangements were left to Mum, she had every right to do things the way she wanted. 'Maybe she just feels like having a rest for once', he said. I'm all for women's lib and not taking people for granted, but what does she think being a mother is all about?

In the end, Jon and I decided to put Christmas together by ourselves – all Mum has to do is cook the turkey. She agreed, a bit grudgingly I thought, considering Jon and Dad and I will be doing all the real work. But at least I have saved some remnant of a proper Christmas for my family. And for George, of course...

19th December

I wish I had thought of pulling out of Christmas years ago. When I suggested that we make some amendments to the traditional blow-out, Jon and Jenny were horrified. They even pledged to do all the work themselves. It won't work out that way, naturally. Still, I was impressed with the thought and planning that went into their joint proposal to 'save the family Christmas' as Jenny put it.

I suppose it was a bit mean to suggest pork chops

32

when I knew Jenny really wanted to impress George on Christmas Day. I had actually only been going to suggest that we might book a restaurant table for one of our Christmas dinners, and that I would buy the puddings and cakes from the shops instead of slaving over the stove. But when Jenny started getting all sanctimonious about tradition and family ties, I couldn't resist taking it all just a bit further. It was so funny. I'm still laughing now when I remember the looks on their faces.

I do plan to hold them to their promise to work like slaves to get everything ready. It will be good for both of them, and especially for Jenny, to appreciate how much work goes in to that one special day they're so keen to hang on to.

19th December

Last day of school at last. The committee were let off afternoon lessons to get the hall ready for the youth centre disco (perhaps they're not so dim after all). George was at college all day but he agreed to come half an hour early in case of last-minute problems. At least he's doing a classroom block, which means he won't have to be on the wards over Christmas.) But I had to spend the afternoon with Louise Ann Maynard and her terminally boring chatter AND her drain gurgling laugh. Sadie came along to help a bit after school, and quite a few teachers and kids drifted in during the afternoon asking where to put things or whether we needed a hand.

The disco was quite good fun, in the end. The hall looked lovely, the food was brilliant (the school caterers did it, but it was nothing like school dinner) and the music wasn't all naff – plenty of smoochy ones for George and me to dance to. Best of all, towards the end, Louise Ann Maynard asked George for a dance and he said he had already promised to dance every single dance with me! When I asked him why he said that – it wasn't true – he said I was the only one he wanted, and he didn't want Louise to get any idea that he and she were more than just friends. Perhaps he's not as dumb as I thought...

Christmas Eve

It's actually Christmas morning, about 1a.m. It hasn't snowed, but it's cold and crisp and Dad says there'll be a thick frost in the morning, which is nearly as good. Mum and Dad went to midnight mass, and I have been cuddling Lizzie back to sleep after one last feed. Jon has finally dropped off after coming down at least four times to tell me Father Christmas hasn't been yet. I suppose this might be the last Christmas he believes in Santa, and then we'll start all over again with Lizzie.

I've been sitting in the dark in Lizzie's room watching her sleep in my arms. The light from the street lamp outside made the room glow, and the night is so quiet and peaceful. Hardly a house in the street has a light on now. As I put Lizzie down in her cot, she stirred a bit and smiled in her sleep. I feel so full of Christmas goodwill I could burst.

It's going to be so special this year, with a baby in the house, and with someone I love to share it all with. George's parents are very religious and I wondered whether they thought Christmas was spoiled by all the tinsel and glitter, but they love it. His mum insists that they are two separate festivals, side by side – the worldly midwinter celebration and the Christian welcome to Jesus. She gets very cross when people try to suggest that you can't have both. I like that point of view. You can dig into your presents and stuff yourself with food and not feel at all guilty. I can't wait.

*The awful boy we call our son awoke at five a.m.
raring to go and determined to make sure none of us
missed a moment of this very special day. He told me
a week ago that he knows there isn't really a Santa,
but he still brought his stocking gifts in to show us as
if we hadn't seen them before. Mike and I tried our
best not to get snappy, although we were both
shattered. Afterwards, Jon agreed to go downstairs
and watch television (thank God for early morning
TV!) and Mike and I snuggled down again. Then
Lizzie woke up, and that was that.*

*Jenny had made a list of things to do and had
insisted we wake her up at eight o'clock. When the
time came she was less than enthusiastic about the
idea, and became quite abusive. Mike and I decided
not to get involved in an argument. She was still in
bed when George came at about ten. Then she was
upset that we had let her sleep, and 'miss half of
Christmas'. She overlooked the fact that she had also
missed the preparation of vegetables, the setting of
the table, and the bathing of Lizzie — all things from
her list for the day which Mike and I had to do.*

*I don't want to sound as though the day was
disappointing, though. It was lovely. The dinner came
together very well, despite Jenny's attempts to
impress George with her culinary skills which resulted
in four attempts at gravy and a very hot, red face at
the dinner table. Lizzie was entranced by all the
wrapping paper, and when Jon saw his new computer
he and Mike disappeared for the rest of the
afternoon. Jenny and George snuggled up together
on the sofa, with their ears plugged into walkmans
while they swapped their new tapes, and Lizzie and I
had a leisurely nap. It was such a change from the
hectic rush we usually have getting everything ready
for guests, or the tiredness of a long journey to visit*

Mum and Dad in Devon. I think we will keep Christmas Day just for us in future.

Jenny was outraged that George had already opened his present from her before he arrived. At his house they open all their presents as soon as they wake up. Jenny is used to having a stocking to keep her going and then having to wait until after lunch for the real presents. They had quite a hot debate over which way is best, but I refused to get involved.

In the evening we all played with the 'Cluedo' Jon got from my parents and then watched the big film. It has been a lovely day, but I'm shattered.

27th December

It's been a really good Christmas – quiet, not particularly exciting, but *nice*. We spent Christmas Day at our house (I helped cook the dinner, which is bound to have impressed George). George bought me a beautiful silver bangle, with my name carved into it saying, 'I Love You'. I bought George a new holdall for college, since his old one's fallen apart. He brought it with him, and said it was great. I was a bit annoyed that he hadn't waited until we were together to open it, but in his house they tear the presents open as soon as they open their eyes. Daft idea, opening your presents first thing. What do you do after dinner?

I found out when we went to George's for Boxing Day. It was certainly a contrast – the noise was non-stop and if you got up for a moment you lost your chair to one of the children. No wonder George is so sweet and gentle – you'd have to go that way or turn into an axe murderer, just to survive.

After dinner Seamus, George's dad, made a speech highlighting the special events of the year. This is one of their family traditions, and it's really sweet. He goes through each member of the family and says nice things about what they've done over the year. Even Adelia, who's only three, got a mention. She learned to go to the loo all by herself this year, and makes a fine jam tart with her mother. She went all giggly – it was so cute. When it was George's turn, his dad looked at me and winked. He said he was proud of George for two things – sticking at nursing despite everyone (including his dad) saying it was a girl's job, and for winning the love of a good woman. Everyone laughed, and I went bright red. Then Seamus started telling a stream of Irish jokes. I tried not to laugh, because they were all racist stereotype ones, but they were too funny. Seamus says it's O.K. to laugh if an Irishman tells Irish jokes, but that doesn't make sense to me. So I said so, and that started a hot debate which ended in us throwing napkins and bits of cracker around. Gran would be horrified, and would be looking at Mum to see what she was going to do. But Alicia just laughed and told the little ones to dive for cover. Our families are so different.

On New Year's Eve Sadie and Adam, Cathy and Ted, and me and George are all going to a restaurant together. It was Cathy's idea. She said she wanted her best friends with her for this particular New Year. Gloria (her mum) still goes to Alcoholics Anonymous and is doing well. She got this job at the restaurant, doing the books and ordering and so on. The owner is someone she met through AA, and he thinks she's really talented, so that's a boost for her. She booked the table, and we all get to eat at staff rates. I suppose the owner must fancy Gloria, and being nice to her daughter is his way of ingratiating himself. I've no complaints. It will be something to look forward to during the visit of the old dears. We've never had Mum AND Dad's parents visiting at the same time before. I have a sneaky feeling they're not going to get on well...

We saw Mum and Dad off on the train this afternoon, and Mike's parents went straight after breakfast. So ended nearly four whole days of unmitigated gloom and tension. By the evening of the first day, Mike's mum had put my mum out of sorts by muscling her out of the kitchen and insisting on doing all the washing up. Mum retaliated by holding Lizzie all the time so that Emily didn't get a look in, and Jon played the two women off against each other quite horribly. Sensing competition in the air, he managed to manipulate both of them into feeding him sweets and drinks almost non-stop. He deserves to be sick, and if he is he won't get any sympathy.

The men were slightly better behaved, but they vote for different political parties, support different cricket teams and while Dad is an addict of soccer, Alec insists that only rugby football has any real merit. That didn't leave room for much male bonding, so they tended to watch television and doze off.

Still, we survived, and we are hoping for a quiet evening toasting in the New Year with Mavis and Donald, who are coming over for dinner. Jon has Carlo over for the night, and Lizzie is her usual cheerful self and hopefully will sleep all evening. Jenny is off to a swish restaurant with some friends. Resolutions? To be more organized, and to manage my time better so that I can be with the children more. I'm sure Jenny will appreciate my help and guidance in her last couple of years at home with us before she flies the nest.

31st December

Ted has left his wife! He and Cathy are moving into a flat

together tomorrow, to start a new life, they tell me. Cathy has found a job in the bank, and will not be going back to school. Ted has actually been living in this flat for a month already, but Cathy didn't want to leave her mum before Christmas because of all the drink that's on offer. I wonder how Ted's wife feels about being left just before Christmas. Ted says it was all over before he met Cathy and it's a relief to both of them to admit it, but then he would say that, wouldn't he?

Sadie and I didn't know where to look when Cathy announced it, for all the world like she was announcing a marriage. (I noticed they were both very careful NOT to say anything about getting married). Adam saved the day by immediately proposing a toast and making a short speech about his hopes for a long and happy future for them both. Sadie said afterwards that Adam had an inkling that they would be telling us this news, so he was better prepared.

I have to be happy for Cathy. You can see she really loves Ted, and I don't suppose she's ever felt quite so settled in her whole life. She will have her own home, without the responsibility of trying to stop her mother from falling off the wagon all the time, and Ted seems to love her too. I just can't make myself like him. There's something about him. George says it's because he's older, and already married, and I'm stuffy about that sort of thing. But it's not that. It just doesn't feel right. When I said that, George laughed. It can be quite irritating, this insensitivity of his.

So we all saw the New Year in together. We had to make a public resolution which the others will make us stick to. Mine was to stop winding Jon up. George said he was going to study harder. Cathy is going to look for a better job, Ted is going to 'make Cathy happier than she's ever been' (yuk!) and Sadie and Adam had the same resolution (of course) which is to save at least half of whatever money they get 'for the future'. Aaah.

I think I had a bit too much wine, and the cocktails

39

beforehand were definitely a mistake. My head is swimming around without my body, and I can't write any more. Happy New Year!

Poor old Mike had to go back to work today. It felt as though we had had almost no time at all for Christmas, and everyone was feeling a bit down at the prospect of office and school. The house was very quiet, and Lizzie was fretful. It seems even babies can suffer the post-Christmas blues!

But all that was completely blown out of the water by Mike's surprise announcement. I could tell he was bursting with something as soon as he got home, but he just hissed that he would tell me later, when the children were out of the way. It was all so mysterious, and so exciting, I'm surprised we got through the next few hours. But in the end Lizzie was bathed and bedded, Jon had had his story and snuggled down, Jenny got stuck into her homework upstairs, and Mike finally spilled the beans.

He has been offered the chance to go to Victoria, in British Columbia, for four months over the summer! And to take his family! Apparently the Managing Director of the Canadian section has heard good things about him (we don't know from whom, but we bless him or her for it). He has asked Mike to come and personally oversee a new computer system they're putting in at their Victoria base. The whole of their business in Canada is going on to the latest networking system. I don't understand it but Mike says it's really exciting — the latest in computer technology on a grand scale, right across the company and it will all cost millions and millions of pounds. They want someone they can really trust to make sure it's done right, and they don't have anyone

40

in British Columbia who has the experience Mike has built up in the European division.

It sounds as though they want Mike a lot. They will get us a house, pay all the expenses of the flights, children's schooling etc. And although it will be a big responsibility, if it all turns out right it will be an incredible achievement and can only further his career. How could we refuse such an offer?

I said yes straight away. Now all we have to do is carefully prepare our ground before we tell the children. I have a sneaky feeling it won't sound quite so wonderful to them as it does to us.

January 12th

There have been times in my life when I have suspected my parents of being lunatics, but when pushed I would have said they fell just about into the ordinary human range. But now I have conclusive proof that they are completely off their trolleys OR they are in fact descended from alien beings, whose ship left without them many moons ago. I can hardly believe I am having to write this down, but my mother and father are planning to ship us all off to Canada for FOUR WHOLE MONTHS! Dad was offered the 'opportunity' of heading some boring computer project. And without a second thought he said yes. Never mind having to take Jon and me out of school, never mind poor little Lizzie learning to talk with a weird accent, never mind my whole life being mucked up because George will find someone else and I won't get my 'A' levels because I will miss most of the course. We don't matter.

I reckon it's some kind of mid-life crisis. Dad senses he's on the scrap heap and he's determined to have one last fling. I did my pieces, but it was no use. I think they had a battle plan all ready. The toad, Jonathon, is quite excited. He can't wait to get to school to tell all his

41

friends. I pointed out that he would be leaving all these
friends behind, and that four months was almost forever.
(I thought Mum was going to wallop me.) But Jon just
shrugged his shoulders and said he would be coming
back to them and besides, he'd bring back some really
good souvenirs to share. He is going to go to school in
Canada – he even thinks that's neat. So no help there.

For every single objection I made, they had an answer.
I said I couldn't miss all that course work. THEY said
they had already talked to the school and that only part
of the trip would be in school time. Mr Downing has said
it would be a wonderful opportunity and he's sure I
would be able to keep up with the work, with a bit of
forward planning. Most of the courses can be done
independently, HE says, and only the Biology practicals
would have to be caught up. So no help there. I told
them they would wreck my chances with George, and
Mum just smiled and said she thought that it was a good
way to find out how we really feel about each other.
Then Dad said that if I was absolutely determined not to
go, they wouldn't make me. That was the cruellest of all,
because just as I was about to say thank you from the
bottom of my heart, he added that Gran and Grandad
had already said that they would come up here to stay
with me, and take me back to Devon once term finished.
It was as if they had everything worked out right from the
start, and knew exactly what I was going to say. I am
speechless about the whole thing, truly speechless.

January 12th

*As anticipated, Jenny's reaction was all shock,
horror, drama, woe is me. Mike and I were superb. We
listened, with our heads slightly on one side and
sympathetic expressions. Then we calmly countered
every hysterical claim with one of our own. For once,
our daughter was outclassed and outgunned. All the*

effort we put in to making sure exactly what would happen about school and so on was well worth the time. Jon asked lots of questions about the school he would be going to, which we could answer because Mike had all the literature on the place. Jenny insisted we would be responsible for her whole career failing if she didn't get her 'A' levels and we told her we had discussed it with the Head of Sixth and he couldn't see any problems.

My parents' kind offer to come and stay with her, though, was the master stroke. I wish I'd had a camera when we told her that. We were being so thoughtful, so democratic. Of course we wouldn't force her, of course she had a choice; she was just that tinsy winsy bit young to be left alone for such a long time. We were even ready for the possibility of her saying she would find a friend's family willing to take her in — now that they had offered, Grandma and Grandpa would be so hurt if she decided to stay in England, but not with them.

In the event, Jenny was too stunned even to think of it. Ah, the rare, sweet scent of victory over a teenage daughter...but I am sure there will be battles to come. In truth, I do feel sorry for her. I am pushing away all the twinges of guilt by telling myself that this will be the last opportunity for a real family trip before Jenny flies the nest. Once she is in Canada, I don't believe she will have any regrets. But the next few weeks will be rough.

14th January

I told Sadie and Cathy about Mum and Dad's plans. They both think it's brilliant. The words were no sooner out of my mouth than they started talking about maybe coming out to see me. Sadie asked if we would have enough room to put them both up. When I said Mum

43

had tried to show me pictures of the house, but that I was refusing to have any discussion about the place whatsoever, they both said I was mad! Sadie said she'd give anything to be in my place – offered to swap lives for four months. When I said what about Adam, she smiled and said their love was strong enough to take a separation, and he would want her to take a chance like that if it was offered. Bring on the sick bucket (but it made me feel a bit bad that I didn't think that way about George and me). Cathy, predictably, looked at it from the man angle. She said I'd have a head start, because all the Canadian boys would go for my accent. She said I'd be exotic over there, whereas over here I'm just ordinary. She's a true friend, I don't think.

I tried to make them understand how awful it would be, and how much I would miss George. Cathy said if I was sure he was going to be the one I ended up with, then it was my bounden duty to have one last fling, and no-one could possibly find out about it if that fling was halfway across the world. Sadie said in any case it would prove one way or the other whether George and I were meant to be. If we lasted four months apart and still loved each other when we got back together, then that would be it.

Neither one of them was any help to me at all. No-one understands how horrible all this is for me. I expect George will, but I haven't plucked up the courage to tell him yet.

16th January

I told George. I had to. He asked me if I wanted to come away on holiday with him in the summer, and I had to tell him why I couldn't. He went very quiet, and then said he thought it would be a great opportunity for me. I think if one more person mentions that word to me I will ram it down their throats, letter by letter.

44

We tried to talk about what we would do to get through the time apart, but we both ended up crying and hanging on to each other like drowning souls. It was awful, but kind of romantic, too. I told him how much I love him, and how unbearable it would be without him. I even said I was willing to live with my grandparents, if that was what he wanted. But George, as always, was really sweet. One of the things I love about him is that he's always so positive. It's like he was born full of sunshine, and it can't help trickling out. He said we could telephone every other day and write every day. He suggested we should start saving to pay the telephone bills, and find out everything we could about where I would be living and what I would be doing so that he could imagine me there. I asked him if he would go out with other people, and he looked so shocked I wish I hadn't said anything.

I should have told George right at the start. He always manages to make me feel better about things. A lot of what he said made sense, even if it agreed with what Mum and Dad have been saying. It will be a good chance to go and see another way of life, and the last one I'll get where all my expenses will be met by someone else. I hadn't thought of that – once I leave school, I suppose I will have to pay for all my holidays. George made me feel like we could survive it, and that when we got back together it would prove to everyone how serious we were. So in the end I felt a lot better about the whole thing. Not that I'm going to tell Mum that, of course. She feels so guilty about all the misery she's heaping up for me that she's being really nice. She's promising all sorts of things that we can do once we're out in Canada, like she said we wouldn't need to take much in the way of clothes because things out there are much cheaper and we may as well take the opportunity to get a whole new wardrobe of stuff that you can't get over here. She's enthusiastic about Sadie and Cathy coming out to stay as well – if they can find the air fare, she'll have them for a couple of weeks for nothing. I think I'll hold out a bit longer before I start to show any enthusiasm – I don't want to miss any other juicy offers.

January 22nd

It's been a long haul but I think Jenny has finally come to terms with the idea of going to Victoria. Last night she actually submitted to being shown the photographs of the place. She and Jon were debating whether they would have large enough bedrooms. Mike says Saanich, where we will be, sounds really nice – one of his colleagues actually lived in the neighbourhood for a few years, and he has been telling Mike all about it. Most of the houses have basements and rooms tend to be larger than English ones – not so worried about heating, I suppose, with fuel about half the price it is here – so I was able to reassure them on that score. We looked at travel brochures together. Mike's secretary had very thoughtfully gathered loads of stuff from the tourist office and from contacts in Canada.

Victoria looks beautiful in itself, but Vancouver Island looks almost magical. It has rain forest, bears, cougars (Jon was particularly fascinated by the idea of wild bears and made us promise we would go looking for some!), ocean, beaches, mountains – everything beautiful the world has to offer seems to be there in one form or another. Jenny said we must go looking for whales – there are several tour centres on the Island which guarantee sightings on their boat trips. I put her to work, with Jon, making a list of the things they thought we should see and do during our time there. For the children and me it will be almost entirely holiday. Jon will go to school for about a month, and my plan is to get Jenny to work very intensively during that time too. Then, even though

Mike will be at work, for the rest of us it will be like a three month holiday. I am so looking forward to it, especially now that Jenny is beginning to show a grudging interest.

2nd February

My life seems to be sinking into an ever deeper mess. I still can't believe that I'm going to have to leave my home and friends behind for four whole months, and all that would be bad enough without my teachers bleeping on and on about how important it will be for me to get ahead before I leave for my 'North American Experience' as Jack J. Jackson puts it. He, of course, has been to Victoria and has also toured British Columbia – 'truly the milk and honey paradise portayed in Biblical epics'. Just knowing that Jackson likes the place is enough to put me right off.

George was very supportive about me going at first, but he has been so ratty lately that I think it must be getting to him really. I'll miss him so badly I don't think I'll be able to stand it. I tried to explain this to Mum, but she just smiled and said she remembered feeling the same way once, and not to worry. How's that supposed to help?

5th February

Mavis called me from Casualty this afternoon. Gloria was brought in unconscious – sleeping pills and alcohol. She was found by a neighbour lying in her garden, of all things. They haven't been able to get hold of either of the children. Cathy is out somewhere, and her brother is on field exercises in Cyprus. The army are arranging to get him home as soon as they can, but it looks as though Gloria is

47

unlikely to survive the night. Poor Cathy; I didn't approve of her moving in with an older man, but at least it looked as though her life was in with a chance of being a bit happier. Now this.

I went up to Casualty: in the absence of her children there is no-one else. Messages have been left for Cathy all over the place. I do hope she makes it to the hospital in time.

Gloria was peaceful but oblivious: I don't think she knew I was there, but I kept talking to her just in case. I told her that Mike and I would look after Cathy as though she were our own, and that she mustn't worry. Mavis came to collect me when her shift finished. She insisted on driving me home. I couldn't even see my way out of the hospital for the tears that kept running down my face. It seems such a waste. Gloria was doing so well – how could this happen? The Consultant says we'll never know whether it was deliberate or not – the overdose wasn't massive, but she'd drunk at least half a bottle of whisky as well, and her organs were already damaged.

Jenny was stunned. She and George are out now, searching for Cathy. It's like looking for a needle in a haystack, but Jenny says she doesn't want Cathy to hear from strangers. They're going to go to every friend and every bar and cinema that Cathy and Ted like to go to. I do hope they find her.

6th February

Once again I have been made to realize how pathetic my own small problems are in this world. Cathy's mum died last night. She seems to have got confused, possibly after getting very drunk, and taken too many sleeping pills. That's what the hospital say, but Cathy seems to believe that her mum committed suicide. Worse than that, Cathy thinks she wouldn't have done it if Cathy had not

48

left home. Her mum was very upset about that, apparently. But I don't think her mum was the type to kill herself. George and I spent ages searching for Cathy to tell her that her mum was in hospital. She was out on a day trip with Ted, and didn't get back until after midnight.

Cathy is in a real mess. She can't stop crying, and keeps shaking. I don't think Ted is being exactly supportive. He looks embarrassed – he puts his arms around her but I don't think he has a clue how to comfort her. He's so used to her being the life and soul of the party that I think it's a bit of a shock to him to find she does have real feelings after all. He even left her at the hospital, just after her mum died, because he was worried that his car park fee had run out and he would get a parking ticket!

9th February

Gloria will be buried tomorrow. Mike and I made all the arrangements. I went round to Gloria's house to sort through her papers. Cathy was sure Gloria had written a will saying what she wanted to happen to everything, but Cathy couldn't bear to enter the house. To my surprise, considering how chaotic Gloria could be when drunk, all her papers were in careful order. There was a will, a life insurance policy, and a letter which set out her preferred funeral arrangements and a list of people to contact. The letter was written when Cathy was sixteen, and says that she is hopefully old enough to look after herself with some financial help. The house will be hers and Gary's – Cathy thought it was rented, but apparently not. The other surprise was that Cathy's father, who as far as I know was never on the scene, was quite wealthy and had set up a trust fund – not a vast amount, but at least she will be able to afford basic

49

upkeep on the house.

There was also a personal letter for each of the children. I'm glad Gloria thought of doing that, and I hope it will be some comfort, especially to Cathy. Gary left home years ago and was seldom in touch. He's only staying for one night before the funeral – he's flying straight back to Cyprus after that. I asked Cathy if she wanted to stay with us, but she prefers to be with Ted. I think he is finding all this very difficult. He confided to me that he had always had a fear of disease and death ever since his own mother died at an early age. Cathy's bereavement is bringing it all back for him, too. He hates talking about it, but you can see he is doing his best to show Cathy how to get through the experience. She is probably better off with him than with us.

10th February

Cathy's very blackest day must surely have been today, her mum's funeral. It even rained constantly. There were quite a few people there from Alcoholics Anonymous, which was nice, but her entire family now only consists of her brother and two cousins whose names she couldn't even remember. Her dad sent a wreath, which was really weird. It was very expensive-looking, and read 'To Gloria, thanks for the good times. Charles.' But he didn't even contact Cathy to make sure she was all right.

Ted is being a real crumb. He said he couldn't get time off work to get to the funeral, and my parents had to arrange everything and have everyone over to our house afterwards. Cathy says he is really loving and supportive when they're alone together, but he can't cope with all the rituals and mourning and stuff. I think he's just out for what he can get. He probably would have been bored of her anyway by now, but since she's come into money it's in his interests to stick around.

He won't listen to all the things Cathy needs to say about her own feelings either. He just kisses her and tells her it will be all right. So I'm the only one she can talk to, she says. I feel a bit weighed down with the responsibility. I'm not a counsellor, and some of the things she's saying are really heavy. She blames herself for her mum dying and she has mixed up emotions about their whole life together, and about her dad as well. I want to help, but I'm scared to death of saying the wrong thing and making things worse.

10th February

Gloria's funeral went well, despite the foul weather, and many friends came to pay their last respects. We had the gathering at our house, to relieve Cathy and Gary of the responsibility. She looked so young and frail as people came to shake her hand on leaving the ceremony, that I wanted to hug her all the time. When I took her home, Ted was waiting anxiously at the window and ran out to meet us. He couldn't face the funeral but he said he wished now that he had gone, because knowing that he had left Cathy to face it all on her own made him feel much worse than being there would have done. He seems a genuinely nice man, and I hope it works out for the two of them.

14th February

I have been spending a lot of time with Cathy the last few days, particularly while Ted has been at work, and I forgot to send George a Valentine card. I felt awful when I saw his card to me lying on the mat. The local shop had sold out, so I couldn't get one until after school, and although I told him I had forgotten to post it, I know George knew I'd simply forgotten. He didn't say

51

anything, but he was a bit quiet all night.

We went out for a drink, and then George insisted on going down to the youth centre disco – all teenyboppers and dreadful music. Apparently Louise Ann Maynard had asked him to come. I thought this was an excellent reason for staying away, but I think he wanted to punish me, so he said he wanted to go. We stayed for three records, and left – but not before Louise Ann Maynard had landed a kiss on my George which looked a bit more than just friendly! I think he could have resisted a bit harder, and I told him so. We haven't exactly rowed over it, but things are a bit frosty between us at the moment.

19th February

Jenny seems to be having a burst of enthusiasm for schoolwork. She is in almost every night, slaving over her books. She says she is trying to get ahead in time for our trip to Canada, but she won't be drawn any further. Where is George? Is he studying too, or are they off at the moment? Jenny's not saying, but they are not telephoning each other constantly any more.

I am trying to organise everything for Canada, which seems to be coming alarmingly close. I only remembered today that Lizzie would have to be added to our passports. I wonder what else there is that has so far been forgotten? Mike says he has a check list at work which is given to all employees going abroad, but he keeps forgetting to bring it home. I finally called his secretary today and asked her to send it.

I suppose in a way it will be good if Jenny and George are no longer an item when we leave. Jenny miserable but available to go out with other boys is a better prospect than Jenny miserable without her man and without the prospect of another. It does seem unduly important to this younger generation to

*be someone's partner. Was it that way in my day? I'm
glad to say I'm too old and too settled to remember.*

20th February

I don't know what's the matter with George. Or perhaps
it's me. Ever since Cathy's mum died we don't seem to
have been the same with each other. I thought he just
resented the time I spent with Cathy, but it can't just be
that. He's not a possessive person, and he could see that
Cathy needed a friend. But then he started forgetting to
phone me, or showed up an hour or so late when we
arranged to meet. I asked him if he had gone off me and
he said no, but I'm not sure I believe him.

Sadie told me that she saw George with Louise Ann
Maynard in town the other day – one of the evenings I
was round at Cathy's. They weren't holding hands or
anything, but they were walking together. Sadie was
surprised I didn't know – you can see she suspects the
worst. Do I just love him so much I'm blind? Or do I love
him so much I see things that aren't there? I wish I could
talk to Mum about it, but she's racing around all the time
these days. If it's not Lizzie then it's transporting Jon
here there and everywhere or getting things ready for
the Canada move. She never seems to have much time
for talking.

22nd February

My seventeenth birthday. George came round straight
from college with a huge bunch of flowers and cinema
tickets. He was all beaming smiles and lovey-dovey, so I
think I must just have been feeling too sorry for myself.
We had a great night out, and talked for ages about
everything under the sun but especially about how much
we love each other. Then we got down to some serious

53

non-verbal communication. George is the best kisser I've ever been out with. Happy Birthday? You bet.

24th February

George and Jenny are once more going around like a couple of bookends. He came on her birthday with smiles and kisses and a date all lined up, and wham! Jenny was back in love. I suppose he must have told her about the girl Mike saw him with in the park. According to Mike's description, she is a very attractive young lady with huge eyes and luscious lips. I suspect it's the girl that I see at youth club sometimes when I drop Jenny off there. She is very involved in community work and has been obviously attracted to George for some time. I've seen her eyeing up George, and I know from the way George smiles back at her that he knows exactly what's going on. When Mike told me he had seen George kissing a girl in the park near his office, it wasn't hard to put two and two together. I wonder how long it's been going on, and how much he has told Jenny? She must know something, or why else would they have been avoiding each other lately? Looks like George has come clean and been forgiven. I don't think I would be so generous in Jenny's shoes. So now the merry-go-round starts again. I hope the other girl (Louise, I think she's called) is not too broken-hearted.

26th February

I have to hand it to Louise Ann Maynard, she is one of life's eternal optimists, and never gives up hope. Just because George has agreed to stay on the youth club committee, which means going to boring old meetings with her and other naff-minded people, she seems to think she's in with a chance. George says to take no notice of her flirting – he doesn't. I should feel sorry for her really. Spending all this time chasing my man means she has no chance with any of the others. All the same, if she moves in on George, I'll scratch her eyes out (isn't that what they say in magazine stories?!).

8th March

Louise Ann Maynard has been behaving really weirdly the last few days. She keeps smiling at me and being over-friendly, in a very smarmy way that gets on my nerves.

George and I haven't been down to the youth centre in ages. For once, George gave in to my idea that we try out some new places together. George is on men's surgical at the moment and it's his hardest ward yet. We're not seeing so much of each other as we want to. He works shifts, and I've got a stinking great pile of coursework to get through. I have got behind again, and Jack J. Jackson is threatening to write home about all the essays I owe him. I do intend to get down to the homework, but there are so many distractions. All my favourite soaps – *all* of them – are running really good storylines at the moment, and if you miss one you lose what's going on.

Also, Cathy comes round a lot. She's looking terrible, not sleeping and rowing with Ted all the time. Looks like the independent life didn't turn out so well after all. At least the house hasn't been sold yet – if things go wrong with Ted she'll still have a roof over her head. Meanwhile I have got to get two biology practicals written up, write three coursework essays for English and set up a history research project (I was planning to do something about medical history and childbirth practices, but I haven't even been to the library yet). I've been trying to do deals with people who are further ahead than me – essay shares or something – but most of my friends are just as far behind as me. Help!

Jenny is talking very earnestly on the telephone about various bits of coursework. It's heartening to see her taking her studies so seriously. She should have no problems with taking time out from school at this rate; she seems to be streaking ahead with her coursework.

George has not been around so much lately. I know he is finding his new ward quite tough, and is studying hard to keep up. That may have helped Jenny's work routine, but I hope what Mike saw going on between him and that other girl has finished. Jenny has already been two-timed once; it would be unfortunate for it to happen again.

March 13th

Today I had a proper going-over from Miss Swarton about my Biology folder. She says I'm not putting enough effort in (granted) and that my coursework is a mess (a bit exaggerated) and that my mind is constantly elsewhere (true). She says she is fed up of me mooning around after boys (cheek!) when I should be contemplating my own independent future. She's a bit of a lefty – the sort of woman my mum distrusts completely – since she has got married but didn't change her maiden name. She also wears dungarees, which my dad says is a sure sign of militant feminism and repressed longing to have male power (dream on, Dad. What male power?).

Anyway, David Slater, the very same little swine who gave me all that heartache last year when he and I were going out together, suddenly popped up in the canteen and offered to help. He's loaned me his practical notes and some really good revision notebooks. His aunty is a Biology teacher, and she tells him what's going to be on the syllabus and helps him keep ahead. I was very suspicious at first, wondering what he was going to get out of all this, but he genuinely does seem to want to help. Maybe he feels guilty about how he treated me, or wants to get back together. No chance. George and I are going through a bit of a difficult patch, with both of us having to work so hard, but I can't see me ever getting that desperate!

March 14th

Sadie came round last night looking like the end of the world was nigh. At first I thought she had broken up with Adam, but it was worse. She says she and Adam saw George at a Chinese takeaway in town ordering for two – and he was with Louise Ann Maynard! That was two days ago, and it's taken her this long to decide she ought to tell me. I could see how hard it was for her, but I was so shocked I couldn't even speak. Then I telephoned George and told him not to bother ever coming near me again, and that Louise Ann Maynard was welcome to him. Then I sobbed all over Sadie and have now declared never, ever, to be sucked in by a boy again. They're all liars and cheats, unless I have the uncanny knack of always attracting the bad ones. We're much better off without men, I reckon. Even talking about them is a waste of time. Mum is going to be gutted when she finds out it's all over between me and George; she really liked him. I'll leave her in blissful ignorance of his betrayal a bit longer. Why spoil everyone else's life? He's not worth it.

*Something is going on. The teenage drama show is
back on the road. Jenny was visited quite late tonight
by Sadie, who had the air of tragedy and anticipation
that you only see on teenagers (or on TV). She clearly
had Significant News to Impart. She and Jenny went
upstairs, and did not surface for a long time, except
for one brief telephone call. When they did emerge
they were both red-eyed and had clearly been going
through some supportive sisterhood experience. I
knew it could only be boy trouble, but they both
looked so doom-laden it was impossible to tell whose
man had done her wrong.*

*I asked Jenny what was up, and she said absolutely
nothing, what on earth made me think something was
the matter, did I think her life revolved around boys,
or what? So it is man trouble, and more likely George
than Sadie's boy. I wonder if George is still seeing that
girl from the park? I think I'll keep my head down –
Jenny will no doubt tell me soon enough, and I'm a
bit tired for all that teenage angst just at the moment.*

George telephoned me today, straight after school. I told
him I did not want to hear any of his excuses and that
there were plenty more fish in the sea, so not to worry
about me. He almost begged me to see him tonight, but
I said I was seeing someone else, and I put the phone
down. Then it hit me that it was a bit stupid to say that,
since I had no-one else to see at all. So I called David
Slater and asked him if I could go over and borrow his
project notes to try and catch up. He sounded surprised,
but suggested we meet at the pub and he would hand
over the notes and buy me a drink if I liked. I not only
said yes, but I told Mum where I was going and with

whom, so that if George called back she could tell him. Poor Mum doesn't even know what's going on between me and George. You could see she was all agog for the gossip, but she tried not to show it.

I met David at the pub and he was really good company and easy to talk to. I ended up telling him all about my troubles. He surprised me by saying that although he didn't know George he knew Louise very well – most of the boys in the Sixth Form know her very well indeed, nudge nudge. She had come on to him and he had told her to get lost. (Apparently he met a girl in France last holiday that he is in love with. They write every day and will be spending the summer together, if he can get a job. Sweet.) We both drowned our lonely sorrows in gallons of Coke (and a couple of ciders) and then I came home feeling a bit better, although I don't know why. I suppose it's easier to believe that Louise was doing all the chasing, even if George didn't have enough strength, or enough love for me, to resist.

March 15th

Jenny is playing with fire. She has obviously had a major row with George, presumably about the other girl, although she is still trying to pretend to me that nothing is going on. George called her tonight. It was a short call, and then she told me she was going off to the pub with, of all people, David Slater, the treacherous ex-boyfriend. I know she told me in the express hope that George would call again, but I pretended to be a bit dense and said I wouldn't let on, then, if George should happen to telephone. She gave me a look, and said no, it was all right to tell him. Just before she left she checked that I knew where she was going. She thinks she is being so devious!

59

Louise Ann Maynard wasn't at school today. Surprise, surprise. George must have told her that I know, and she can't face me. She'll have to come back some time...

George was waiting for me after school. Sadie and Adam told him to shove off. I just ignored him and kept walking. But he followed us, and said he'd taken time off work and would probably be in trouble but he had to tell me the truth. Eventually I let Sadie and Adam go on ahead and I said he could have five minutes (it was quite good, that line. I felt like a film star. 'Five minutes and then you're gone out of my life for ever', I said).

I am so glad that I listened. If I had been as angry as I had felt last night, my whole life would still be in ruins. But now I know that George loves me and never felt anything for Louise Ann Maynard, even though she sunk her nasty little hooks in so deep it was almost impossible to resist.

George is not very bright when it comes to women. He thinks it's all his fault, that he got carried away and gave in to temptation. But listening to him talk you can read between the lines and see Louise at work every step of the way. First she persuaded him to go on the youth centre committee with her, and got him involved in all kinds of things which meant they had to spend time together. Then she started telling him all her problems, and cooked up stories of how unhappy she was at home etc. etc. George, who is the happiest family person I know, obviously felt terrible about all this and tried to help by listening and giving her support. He says he just sort of felt entangled. He kissed her a couple of times because he felt sorry for her, and they held hands and went out together to talk in private. George insists it wasn't a date, just finding somewhere private to talk properly when Louise Ann Maynard was 'upset'. I can see it all now.

I am angry with George for being so stupid, but I do

believe him. He was so bewildered by my anger about him being seen with that foul piece of goods, so worried that I would get the wrong idea and dump him, that I couldn't not believe him. He has promised to stay well away from the youth centre. He has already told Louise Ann Maynard that he can't see her any more because I might get the wrong idea and think there's something going on. I bet she loved that bit.

I telephoned Sadie and let her know. She sounded as relieved as I am!

18th March

Louise Ann Maynard finally showed up today. She's had an ear and throat infection, apparently. Shame it wasn't something worse. I tried to find her at lunchtime and both breaks, but she managed to avoid me. It was agony sitting all through lessons watching her and not being able to say anything. As she left English this afternoon I caught her at the door and told her I knew all about her little tricks. She said, 'George told you about us then?' as if he and she were still together. When I told her I knew nothing had happened and George had told her to stay clear, she smiled and said, 'Oh, that's what he told you is it?'

I am really ashamed of the next bit, but I must write it down so that I can remember what a stupid idiot I was in times to come, and hopefully not do it again. I shoved her up against the wall and told her she was a liar if she was going to claim there was anything going on between her and George. She said who could blame him for wanting a sophisticated woman instead of a wild little schoolgirl? Then I slapped her, hard, around the face and suddenly we were fighting right there in the corridor. I was aware of people grabbing hold of me and trying to pull me away, and Jack J. Jackson yelling something in the background, but all I could see was this red blur.

61

Finally someone yanked me by the hair and I let go of Louise. We both looked a real mess. Jackson spluttered and hissed like a little furry animal, and hauled us both off to the Head.

He's going to talk to our form tutors and decide what to do. Jack J. Jackson said it was an unprovoked attack on Louise and that I was also abusive to him when he tried to separate us. I won't be suspended, but he'll almost certainly write home.

Mum and Dad will kill me when they find out what I've done. I don't know what came over me. I don't know how I'll ever live it down at school either – it will be all round the place by tomorrow. Even the satisfaction of seeing Louise Ann Maynard with a bloody nose and tufts of hair missing does not compensate for the shame and degradation I'm going to face once it all comes out. My only hope is to keep a very low profile and not give Mum or Dad any aggravation about anything for the rest of my life. Maybe they'll accept a plea of temporary insanity.

George came round tonight to comfort me. Sadie phoned him to tell him what happened. He was really upset and said it was his fault really and he should be the one taking the blame. He even offered to speak to the Head, and Mum and Dad, to tell them what had happened. I told him not to do that, and I was willing to bear all this tribulation to show how much I loved him and trusted his version of what happened between him and Maneater Maynard. I can bear anything, as long as I have George.

19th March

Bring on the clowns, get ready for the grand performance. Our house is so full of sweetness and light and love's young dream that I am deeply suspicious. Whatever it is Jenny has been up to, it's clearly serious. She is studying hard, voluntarily clearing the table and washing up, and offering to amuse Lizzie while I put my feet up. She is even being nice to Jon, and all this without a single threat or bribe. Mike and I are not sure whether it's something she wants, or something she's done. Time will tell.

Jenny has clearly forgiven George for his lapse with the other girl and they are all lovey-dovey again.

Lizzie is beginning to wobble about a bit, getting ready to crawl. She doesn't travel very far but she looks so pleased with herself you can't help laughing. I suppose we had better start putting things on higher shelves. The time seems to have gone so fast. Mike is having many meetings at work setting up the Canadian project. He's quite excited about it. So am I, except for the nerves about getting everything ready. We have agreed to let the house to one of Mike's colleagues from Germany who's going to bring his family over while he sets up a research team for some European Community Initiative. This means the house will have to be spick and span clean, rather than be left in the sort of muddle we usually create immediately before a trip away. I hope I get organized in time.

March 25th

All has become clear. I now know why Jenny has been so extraordinarily sweet these past few days. According to Jon, whose friend Leroy's sister goes to Jenny's school, Jenny had a fight with one of the girls in her English class. (I had to pay Jon fifty pence to get the full details!) A real tears and fists fight it was, with Jenny doing most of the fighting. I gather the other girl came away with a bloody nose. Presumably this was the one Mike saw kissing George in the park.

Of course I am shocked that our daughter should revert to such animal behaviour. But I wish I could

63

*have seen it. A really good fight was such an
entertainment when I was at school. It became part of
the school's folklore, and you could retell the
experience years afterwards. I wonder if this incident
will go into the annals of fame?*

*I have told Mike, but we have decided not to let on
that we know. For a start, the lack of any information
from Jenny herself seems to indicate that she is truly
ashamed of what she did. And, more to the point, I'm
convinced that's why Jenny is being such a paragon of
virtue. Why would we risk losing all that unpaid
labour, the cups of tea, the sweet smiles and
encouragement to the little ones? Not to mention the
concern to get homework done, which makes a nice
change. She's probably learned her lesson.*

March 29th

I seem to have got away with the Louise Ann Maynard
affair. The Head didn't write home. He just gave me a
rollicking that went on for ages and a stern warning that
I would be suspended next time. I've also got a timetable
of extra work to hand in, to make up for all the pieces I
haven't done and extra ones to get me ahead for when
we go to Canada. He says if I miss a single deadline he's
going to write to Mum and Dad and call a meeting about
me.

The cause of all the trouble has not got off scot free,
either. Not only has she lost friends over the way she
tried to steal George, but Jack J. Jackson has decided
she's vulnerable and has appointed himself some sort of
unofficial guardian. She's seeing him quite regularly to
talk things over and make sure she's O.K. That has to be
worse than any punishment I've got!

The only blight is my darling little brother, who
somehow knows all about the fight (probably from
Leroy, who will no doubt be a first class mobster when

he grows up). I had to pay Jon five pounds not to spill the beans to Mum and Dad. George insisted on paying half of it. I do love him.

3rd April

I can't believe it's April already. It seems like just a few days since Dad announced that he was going to transport us all to Canada. One more month, and then I have to leave George behind for what feels like forever. What if one of us dies, or is badly injured? Worse still, what if Louise Ann Maynard makes another move? I trust George completely, but I know his limitations and I don't trust that maneater one millimetre.

It is so selfish of Dad to just take off and leave like that, and expect the whole family to follow in his wake like a cartload of possessions. It's not fair to make Lizzie leave behind her familiar home and toys and smells and sounds and have to adapt to a completely new climate. Mum is trying her best to pretend that she's keen, but she's looking completely frazzled with the worry of it. It's only Dad and Jon who really want to go. Trust the male of the species not to think anything through.

George has asked me to go away for a few days over the Easter holiday with his family. They've got a caravan by the sea – sounds a bit of a squash, but George will go even if I don't and I can't bear to be parted before I have to fly out to Canada.

Jon is being a little pest. I found out yesterday that despite my having paid him a fiver for keeping quiet about the little dispute I had with Louise Ann Maynard, he told Mum anyway! The evil little creature can't even stick to a blackmailer's dodgy bargain. What's more, he wouldn't give me the money back, and when I took action to retrieve what is, after all, rightfully mine, he went crying to Mum who said I had no right to try and bribe him to be quiet in the first place and therefore no right to claim back the money now that he had done the right thing in telling. He's bugging me all the time with his gleeful smile and waving the five pound note under my nose. I am doing my best to ignore him, but I'm feeling quite violent.

I expected Mum to go on and on about the fight but she didn't. She must have got hold of some new psychology book. She just asked me if I felt the fight had achieved anything. I said no, and that was it. In a way I'd have preferred her to do her usual long lecture; at least I could have argued back. But this way I just feel like I was really stupid. Which I was, so I suppose that's fair.

5th April

I am so excited about our forthcoming trip that I can hardly sleep. It's going to be fabulous, and I can't wait to get there. In the meantime I am caught in the middle of a whirlwind of packing, cleaning, shopping and laundry. I want everything to be just right for the family who will be using our house, and I don't want to come back to a load of chores left undone either. So it's all very busy. Mike is doing his best to help, but I feel a bit guilty just throwing Lizzie into his arms as soon as he walks through the door.

Jenny and Jon are showing signs of stress about leaving, too, so they can't be relied upon for very much help. They seem to be bickering all the time, and never about anything important – low-grade, niggling arguments go on constantly. I just ignore them as far as possible. Jenny really blew her top a couple of days ago when she found that I knew about the fight at school. Apparently she had paid Jon to keep quiet, and she demanded her money back, for all the world as though she'd bought faulty goods in a shop. She kept spluttering about 'rights' and 'deals' and when I pointed out that you couldn't legally be held to an illegal contract she went sort of purple and slammed her bedroom door so hard I feared for its hinges. It was very amusing at the time, but her mood has gone from bad to worse since then. We haven't even talked about the fight at school. With her in this mood, there's no point. She's impossible at the moment. I hope George is as patient as he looks.

7th April

George says I'm impossible! Just because I didn't take too kindly to the way he was eyeing up a pretty girl at the bar in the pub he reckons I'm flipping my lid. He told Sadie and Adam that I poured his lager all over him, but there was only a little bit left in the glass and hardly any of it dripped out of his hair. No-one seems to be behaving reasonably at the moment, except me. Mum says that's a sure sign that I'm the one at fault, but of course she would say that, wouldn't she? She's been going around like the wicked queen in a fairy story – do this, don't do that, fetch this, order that. I'll be glad to get away from her, even if it does mean squashing up with dozens of assorted people from George's family.

Jon and his disgusting little friends raided my make-up this afternoon, to try out some war paint designs. My best 'burnished Autumn' lipsticks (I bought two brand new to take to Canada) are a broken-up mess, and there are smears all over my pillow – the creature took his friends into MY bedroom, knowing full well that I would never let him do that if I was here, and knowing too that I would be round at Cathy's until dinner time. What do Mum and Dad do? Just about nothing, as usual. They told him he was a very naughty little boy, and Dad said he'd have to buy another lipstick for me out of his pocket money. He should have been made to really suffer, but they're so busy moaning at me they don't have time to sort him out.

My life is all going wrong, and I don't know how to stop it. The trip to Canada is hovering over me like a massive black cloud and I can't get away from it, and it rains on everything I try to do. George and I were talking about seeing other people while we are away. He said it would be wrong to make me commit myself to being faithful, and he would understand if I would rather see this time apart as a time to meet other people and test out how we really feel about each other.

At the time, I felt so hurt and angry that I said yes, fine, that was exactly how I felt and he should feel free to see other people too. We both smiled at each other and pretended it didn't mean anything but I felt gutted that he could even think about seeing other girls while I'm away. It's not that I think he'll sleep around or anything. We've talked a lot about the attitude people like Cathy have, that you can have sex with anybody whenever you feel like it. I know George thinks she's got it wrong. He says it's important to wait until you're sure about someone. He says it's because his family are Catholic that he's been brought up to feel like that, but I think it's really nice, especially as we are quite sure about our feelings for each other. I know he wouldn't go that far while I'm away, but why would he want to even go out with someone else? Won't he miss me at all?

Mum reckons that he might have been hoping that I would say nonsense, of course I wouldn't be interested in anyone else and, looking back, I think she's right. But it's too late to do anything now, isn't it? I mean, I can't tell him I didn't mean what I said, because what if he DID mean what he said? So I'll just have to hope he didn't mean it. The evening certainly went downhill from that point, and we ended up having a big row. We kissed and made up by the time I got home, but it doesn't feel right. Being on holiday is going to be awful if there's an atmosphere between us.

No way could I even look at another boy, never mind what Cathy says. This trip is wasted on me – it would be a trip to Paradise for her. She's still with Ted but the way she talks makes it sound as though she's even beginning to get bored of him. She's seen someone at work that she really likes. The thought of all those hunky Canadian men sends shivers down her spine, she says. She and Sadie and Adam can't understand how much I DON'T want to go to Canada. They all think it's going to be great.

Jon is driving me round the bend begging me to play his stupid computer games with him, and even Lizzie's little face crumples more often than not when I pick her up. I seem to be surrounded by bad vibes or karma or something. Nothing goes right for me at all any more.

13th April

The children are home for the Easter holidays and that will be it before September for them now; it won't be worth going back at the end of the break for three or four days before we have to leave again. Jenny has gone off to George's family retreat for a couple of days and I'm ashamed to say I'm very relieved to see her go. She has been like a bear with a sore head for days now. No-one can do anything right, especially Jon. He reacts to her impatience by putting special efforts into winding her up, and she blows and he comes running to me...I am so tired of them both I could cheerfully move house permanently and leave them to it. Lizzie is sensitive to atmosphere, and is always miserable when she senses tension in the house. So what with the three of them, and Mike due to fly to Paris for an important convention that he's getting quite stressed about, life in this house is no fun at all.

Tonight George and I walked hand in hand on the beach at sunset, and he told me he could never love anyone else but me. It was so romantic. We wrote our names in the sand, and paddled in the edge of the ocean, and kissed as the waves rolled in on us. It would have been just perfect if it hadn't been for that awful knot in my stomach which tightens every time I think about leaving him. I'm not sure I can survive. I think I might be about to find out whether you really can die from a broken heart.

I bought George a big stationery pack from the gift shop on the caravan site, and he bought me a pen! We both did it separately, to make sure the other person was reminded to write often. It's uncanny how close we are.

George's dad bought the caravan we're in when there were only three children, so it is a bit squashed. But they also have a tent on the little plot of land that goes with the caravan, and the boys go in there with their dad. Alicia and I are in the caravan with the little girls. They are so cute. I'd swop all of them for my one little brother any day. I told Alicia this and she laughed and said I would appreciate Jon when he got older. She said boys are much more trouble than girls when they're little, but when they're grown they're a real joy. I'll take her word for that. She wishes she'd had more sons, although she clearly loves her girls to pieces. I only wish it was in my power to hand Jon over to her for adoption; she'd be most welcome to him.

We have to go home tomorrow. I wish I could stay forever, and watch the sun come up every morning with George. What am I going to do when we're on opposite sides of the world?

15th April

Jenny's back, and don't we all know it. Our little oasis of peace has disappeared like a mirage, and she and Jon are at it hammer and tongs as usual. I am making supreme efforts to keep calm and float above it, but I wouldn't be surprised if I didn't soon start to dream about drowning them both.

20th April

Jon had an accident a couple of days ago which gave us all a terrible scare. I was down at the shops with Lizzie and Jenny was doing her homework at the time, so we aren't clear what exactly happened, but he somehow managed to fall out of the upstairs window. He was unconscious when Jenny reached him, but at least she had the wit to send for the ambulance and not try to move him. I'll never forget the sight that greeted me as I pushed the pram up the road and saw the flashing blue lights parked outside our house. My heart races when I think about it, and whenever I close my eyes I see Jon's still, white little face.

I don't know what I would have done without Jenny. She was so calm. She took Lizzie from me and told me to get in the ambulance and call when there was news. She flinched as she watched Jon's neck and limbs being immobilised as he was loaded onto the stretcher, but she just kept telling me he would be fine. As they took him into the ambulance, Jon regained consciousness. He was terrified and obviously in pain, and started screaming. Jenny calmed him down, and told me quite sternly to stop sobbing or I'd be no use at the hospital and I'd have to stay behind with Lizzie and send her instead. She felt like my mother, not my daughter, but I am so

71

grateful to her now.

Miraculously, Jon had only mild concussion and some cuts and bruises. They kept him overnight – Mike is in Paris and couldn't be reached until late last night so again, Jenny was marvellous and just took over at home so that I could stay at the hospital. Now Jon looks as right as rain. He can't remember what happened. He thinks he was measuring the distance from the window to the ground with a piece of string, but he can't remember why he would want to do that. I'm just thankful it wasn't worse.

Mike brought back a very sophisticated little black dress from Paris as a special thank you to Jenny from both of us. She looks wonderful in it – I just hope George can rake up the money to take her somewhere stylish enough to do it justice.

20th April

I think I must be one of the most selfish, horrible people that ever walked the earth. And now I've had to pay for the rotten way I've been treating Jon the last few weeks. He's only a little boy, doing what little boys do, but I've been so mean to him. I got more and more wound up until I even wished he was dead. Then he fell out of the window in his room and nearly was, and I just can't forgive myself.

I was in my room trying to finish a ton of Biology notes and I could hear Jon calling me. He wanted me to come and help him with something. I ignored him at first, but he kept on and on and in the end I yelled at him to get lost. A couple of minutes later there was this strangled scream. I ignored that too, thinking it must be one of his stupid games. I was supposed to go running out to see what was wrong, and that was the very reason I didn't move from my chair. I wasn't going to give him the satisfaction. It was only when things went very quiet that I went off to see what he was up to. I expected to find him doing something naughty. He wasn't in his room, he wasn't anywhere...then I saw him lying outside. You could tell just by looking at him that he wasn't playing. I honestly thought he was dead.

Everything that happened after that is like a dream. I know I called the ambulance and tried to call Dad in Paris (I had to leave a message at his hotel). Then Mum came and I took Lizzie and she went to the hospital, but I was completely numb. It was only much later, when I had settled Lizzie for the night and Mum had phoned to say they were keeping Jon in but he was going to be fine, that I started to shake and cry. It was just as well that Mum had thought of calling George from the hospital and asking him to come and stay with me. He knew what to do when I started to cave in – he made me a drink and wrapped me in one of Lizzie's blankets and just held me. It was probably the most awful night of my life. If I hadn't been so mean I would have gone to help Jon with whatever little childish thing it was he wanted to do, and he wouldn't have been hurt.

Thank God he's O.K. He looked very small and white when he came home from the hospital, and he still isn't very lively. He sits and watches TV a lot, but the doctor says he'll be right as rain in a few days when he gets over the shock of it all.

One of the worst things about the whole experience was Mum and Dad thanking me for being so helpful. Mum said she didn't know how she would have coped without Dad if it weren't for me, and Dad bought me this gorgeous present – a real French cocktail dress. He saw it in a shop window and said he knew it was just right – amazingly for Dad, whose taste stinks – and he even got the size right. I could tell it was really expensive, and he said it was a special thank you gift for holding the family together.

I don't deserve the dress, and I especially don't deserve to be thanked. I probably caused Jon's accident

73

in the first place. I feel dreadful, and I can't bring myself to tell Mum what really happened. She is so proud of me, and she's telling all her friends. I'm almost glad we're going to Canada now. At least I'll get away from everyone treating me like some kind of heroine.

24th April

One week to go! Jon's accident put preparations a bit behind, but Mike has taken four days off to sort out some paperwork at home, so at least I can leave the children with him while I go out and about. Jon is quite his old chirpy self again now. In a curious way the accident seems to have resolved the problems he and Jenny were having before it happened. She can't do enough for him; the accident obviously gave her a real scare and made her realize how much she loves him and what it would have meant to lose the little chap. She told me yesterday that she really thought he was dead when she first saw him lying on the ground. Poor Jenny. I can imagine how it must have felt. It makes it all the more remarkable that she stayed so calm. Jon appreciates her much more, too, and he doesn't follow her around. Since she is actually offering to play games with him, he's happy to wait until she has time free and comes looking for him.

I am getting to the end of all the spring cleaning. I haven't seen our house looking this clean and tidy since before Jon was born. Almost every room is clean at one and the same time! Usually, when upstairs is clean and tidy downstairs looks like a war zone, and vice versa. I'm almost sorry to leave it. I hope Mike's German colleagues appreciate my efforts – and I hope our house in Canada is as clean as this, because I couldn't face doing it all again!

74

George and I have been spending as much time as we possibly can together before I have to go. Tonight was our last proper date. We went out for dinner to a fairly posh place, and I wore my new black dress. George said I looked really beautiful (his actual words were, 'Well, you scrub up real nice,' but I knew what he meant!) and he looked as gorgeous as I've ever seen him.

Tonight was a night for looking at the stars and making solemn vows. I said he was the only person I could ever be serious about but if he wanted to fill the lonely hours with another companion until I got back, I'd understand – as long as it wasn't Louise Ann Maynard. He promised to stay away from her, and said he hoped I wouldn't get all swoony over some young suntanned Canadian. We both laughed at that. We have both agreed that we couldn't possibly promise to be faithful for that length of time and in the face of such an unknown future, but we are going to write almost every day. When we get back together in September it will either be forever or we will know that it wasn't to be. That's exciting and scary at the same time.

30th April

That's it. The last corner has been cleaned, the last case has been packed. The bills have been paid, instructions left with all the right people about mail and so on. The papers and milk have been cancelled, and food for the fish has been stockpiled. A car has been booked to take us to the airport at the crack of dawn tomorrow. I can officially declare us ready for the trip of a lifetime. Here goes...

We arrived at the hotel at about mid-day yesterday. At least, that's what the clock said. My body wasn't prepared to accept that at all. It was still night-time back in London. I didn't know whether to eat, sleep, have a bath, or simply throw myself off the roof. Most of all, I wanted to go HOME!

Dad suggested that we try and last out until Toronto bedtimes, and after a shower and change he was raring to go round the city and Mum was keen to see the shops. Jonathon and I just wanted to sleep, but Dad insisted that the way to beat the time difference was to a) pretend it didn't exist and b) keep drinking fluids. So he dragged us out anyway. Lizzie, of course, didn't understand all that stuff about pretending there was no time difference. To her, it was time to be asleep, and that was that. She slept in her buggy all afternoon and most of the evening, and woke up full of smiles ready to start her day just as Dad had agreed we could go to bed!

The hotel is quite cute – it's supposed be very European. To a Canadian, 'European' seems to mean lots of palms in pots and fake wood panelling, and curtains that only cover half the window. Funny stuff. Anyway, the woman on reception was very nice, and cooed over Lizzie and offered Jon a sweet. He put his hands behind his back and said 'NO THANKYOU' very loudly and walked away. I remember that stranger danger lesson at school (you can tell he's in Miss Falkdon's class now!). He must have done it just before we left. I would never have had the guts to actually put all that stuff into practice. But Jon had been told not to accept sweets from strangers, and so he wouldn't accept sweets from this stranger. Mum didn't look too impressed, though – she told him off later, for being rude!

I have offered to get up with Lizzie tonight, if she wakes again. She still doesn't understand what time it is.

Anyway, I figure that Mum and Dad wouldn't dare complain about me staying in bed all day tomorrow if I'd done the noble thing and saved them from a broken night tonight. Cunning, huh?

May 2nd

The flight was not as bad as I had expected it to be. Lizzie stayed quite cheerfully occupied with her bag of toys, and only got fractious once or twice. She slept for a lot of the time, which was really useful. Jon enjoyed wandering up and down, watching the stewards at work. They were really good with him, and even let him help with giving things out. He loved the films and having his own personal headset etc. Jenny, after casing the plane for eligible young men and finding none to her liking, snarled something derogatory about the choice of in-flight films, planted her headset firmly on her head and tuned in to a pop music channel while perusing a selection of teenage magazines whose covers promised to change her life. I wish.

The 'Hotel Parisienne' is a cheerful, welcoming place. It will be just the right environment for us to catch our breath before we move on to our house in Victoria. Everyone here has been so friendly – although I don't know what they make of us after Jon's rudeness to the receptionist when we arrived. She offered Jon a sweet and said something about him being a cute little boy. He looked at her as though she were a germ, and pointedly walked away. I suppose he is getting a bit old to be called cute, but still...

I thought Jenny would be very difficult about having to come away with us, but she seems to have mellowed a bit already. Lizzie has had a hard time adjusting to the change in hours, and Jenny has

*offered to look after her tonight if she wakes. She can
see how tired Mike and I are, and Mike has to attend
some very important meetings over the next few days
so a good night's sleep is essential. I'm glad she has
the maturity and generosity to see all that, and to
chip in to help.*

May 3rd

My cunning ploy didn't work. Not only did Lizzie wake
up at four o'clock this morning wanting her breakfast,
but Mum dragged me out of bed at ten anyway, with this
ghastly cheery enthusiasm. I waited for the dreaded word
'museum' – she always heads for a museum wherever
we go – but at least she had the sense to suggest we go
shopping again while Dad took Jon out to a children's
science exhibition.

One thing you have to understand about Canada. It's
big. Huge. They have everything we have, but more of
it. Roads? Their minor roads are more like our
motorways. Cars? Their small cars would make Friends
of the Earth wince. And on almost every corner (or
'block' as they say here, is a shopping centre (mall). So
Mum and I could spend a whole day shopping and not
run out of places to go. Now in London, that would be
bliss. But here, they don't like you to have too good a
time, or perhaps they're worried about crowd control if
you stay too long. So they make sure you're surrounded
by really irritating people.

Once you have fought your way past the greeter, who
accosts you at the door with a huge smile and trots off to
get you a basket, everyone is really nice. Nice. Really.
Nothing is too much trouble. And they smile ALL the
time, like synchronized swimmers. They show you
alternatives, offer to fetch and carry from the changing
room, and chat to you as if you're a friend. Why can't
they prop up the counter and talk about TV and snarl at

78

everyone, like proper shop assistants? Perhaps they ought to do some of their training in England, then they'd get the hang of the atmosphere a really good shop should have.

We got back to the hotel laden with goodies – clothes, table linen, stationery, loads of stuff for everyone. Mum went mad – she says everything's much cheaper here. I bought a couple of CDs that I'd never be able to afford in England – I hope the house we're going to has a CD player. But on the whole, I'm not a big fan of shopping here. On top of everything else, there's the tax. The price you see on something is not the price you pay for it. When you take it to the till, they add tax. So although a Pepsi seems to cost ninety cents, by the time you've paid it's over a dollar. (Mind you, even then a Big Mac, Pepsi and fries only costs half as much here, so Canada does have something going for it.)

We all agreed tonight that our bodies have started to forget English time. I called home twice this evening, to Sadie and to George. Sadie said school is as boring as ever, and I wasn't missing much. She kept me up to date with *Eastenders* and *Neighbours*, but we couldn't talk for long because of the phone bill. George is missing me very much, he says, and although we agreed we'd both feel free to go out with other people, he said he didn't think he'd find anyone like me. Isn't that lovely? It made me feel bad about even looking at the waiter who winked at me last night. I'm going to stay faithful (but I didn't tell George that, just in case).

May 3rd

I can't believe how wonderful shopping is here: you can shop all day and still feel ready for more. The shops are large and airy, there's always room to park and everyone is so helpful. Jenny and I went a bit mad, and came back laden with all sorts of bargains.

Jenny could hardly believe her eyes, either, and was a bit overwhelmed by the experience; either that, or she finds it hard to keep up with her aged mother!

When we got back to the hotel Mike took one look at the bags and boxes and demanded to see the credit card stubs. But the prices here are so reasonable, even he couldn't say too much – not that that stopped him trying. For instance, he doesn't feel Lizzie needs more than a couple of sun bonnets, but they were all so cute I had to ration myself to the six or seven I did buy. Anyway, it does get very hot here, and a bonnet a day when you only want to do the laundry once a week seems entirely reasonable.

Jon very much liked his teeshirts, all decorated with strange alien beings that he watches on television back in England. I sometimes wonder how this generation of children is going to turn out – will they recognize human faces when they go looking for life-long partners, or will they all be drawn to mutated beings from other planets, because people their own age look so boring in comparison? Gruesome thought. Time for a drink, dinner and a long bath – with someone else doing the cooking and cleaning up. I could get used to hotel life, I really could.

May 6th

Dad finished his meetings a day earlier than he expected, which was a nice surprise. You can tell he's raring to go and can't wait to reach Victoria and get stuck in. Once Lizzie and Jon were asleep he opened up a bottle of wine and started to tell me and Mum all about it. Now, when Dad gets enthusiastic about computers, there's no stopping him. He forgets that neither Mum nor I have the faintest interest in the things, and can't understand a word he says. Or maybe he doesn't forget, but doesn't care. I gather yet another new technological age has begun. This thing he has come to Canada to help set up is a huge leap forward. Don't ask me why, although Dad did tell me, in great detail. The people who keep saying that it's the kids who understand computers and the old fogies who get left behind haven't met my dad and me. Any day now I expect computers to be washing up and cooking the dinner while playing 'Amazing Grace' on the bagpipes.

Anyway, we all set off to see Dad's Uncle Jack and Aunty Mave, who live an hour or so away from Toronto. I had never met them before and only knew them as people who sent Christmas cards and nice presents every year. Dad took one of the company's cars (and our lives into his hands) and off we went to pay them a visit. We were supposed to be going for an early evening dinner and then travelling back. But Dad got too drunk to drive, and Mum said she wasn't ready to chance driving on the wrong side of the road.

The thing is, Uncle Jack has a huge bar which he built down in the cellar. It's as big as a pub, and has a snooker table in it as well. So of course, being nothing but a big kid, it was only a matter of minutes before Dad was down there, snooker cue in one hand and a pint in the other. Uncle Jack brews all the beers himself. Dad says they're very professional, and the taste is impressive. I expect that's why he had to try out so many. Jon and I swam in their heated pool. Dinner was served on the patio overlooking the garden (very swish). Dad and Uncle Jack were looking very pleased with themselves by then, and Dad swayed slightly as we sat down. Then there was the wine with the meal...

After dinner Mum and Aunty Mave went in to fuss over Lizzie and have a good natter and Jon and I swam again. It was cold outside by then, but the water was quite warm once you'd been brave enough to take your clothes off. I've never swum in the dark before and it was neat. Finally, Mum said it was getting so late, and Dad was so 'tired' that Aunty Mave had insisted we stay the night and was sorting out towels and spare toothbrushes.

Don't get me wrong, I have no objection to being spoilt rotten by relatives, fed up to the eyeballs and then given a comfortable bed. But isn't it typical parent stuff that if I ever dared to get a bit tipsy, my life wouldn't be worth living and I'd get all the lectures about irresponsible behaviour etc. etc. Yet there's Dad, an old man with family responsibilities who's supposed to set an example getting sozzled out of his skull and no-one bats an eyelid; they just say he's 'tired'. Huh.

May 6th

Mike has finished all the preparations for his project. You could see it was a load off his mind, and he finished ahead of schedule, so until we leave for Victoria, he's all ours. It will give him a chance to unwind a bit before he starts the really hectic business.

We visited Jack and Mave in Mississauga yesterday. We were only supposed to be spending the day there, but they made us so welcome it was hard to leave, and we gladly took them up on their offer of a bed overnight. We had a wonderful time. They have a pool in the garden and the children were thrilled with it. Mave says the weather is unexpectedly warm for May, but it didn't feel quite warm enough to me for swimming so the children had it all to themselves. Jack is a very keen amateur brewer, and he and Mike had a grand old time comparing brews and flavours (and, in truth, sampling quite a few, too). It was just what Mike needed after all the pressure leading up to leaving the Europe office and getting here with basically nothing to build from. He had a chance to unwind and really relax, and finally fell asleep over the snooker table. It was just as well we didn't have to drive back; he was too exhausted. As for Mave and I, we talked and talked for hours (Mave has more stamina than me on that score, but it was so entertaining I managed to keep my eyes open). We had a tour of the local sights before returning to the hotel. We will see Mave and Jack tomorrow, when we meet up at Niagara for our last outing before we leave Toronto. I have been looking forward to seeing the falls ever since we knew we would be coming to Canada, but I was very keen to see them with Mike, so we had to leave them until last.

Lizzie is now sleeping peacefully, having got used to the different times. I expect it will all go haywire again when we get to Victoria, where there's a three hour difference. I'm not looking forward to that, but it will be nice to be settled into a more permanent base. Tomorrow we will be spending our last day in this part of Canada – and what better way to finish than to visit Niagara Falls?

May 7th

I have always wanted to see the Falls, and was not disappointed. They are spectacular, even allowing for the inevitable ring-around of tourist accoutrements. You can hear and taste them: the water thunders down with such force that the spray drifts quite some distance.

It was quite a warm day, and no-one had much energy for walking, which was a shame. Also, Jon was not feeling well, probably because of the very smooth car ride and the heat, and he had been sick (very neatly, into a plastic carrier bag!) in the car on the way. We didn't feel it would be appropriate to take the hop-on, hop-off bus which ferries you around the attractions in the area, just in case. We decided to take a trip on the 'Maid of the Mist' instead. This boat goes right into the centre of the Falls. We left Lizzie chuckling away in the arms of Aunty Mave, and Jenny very sweetly volunteered to stay behind too, to look after Jon. Surprisingly, Jon said he didn't feel sick any more and wanted to go with us, so we set off together.

The company running the enterprise thoughtfully provided huge blue plastic macs – not much more than sheets of polythene, really, but you can apparently get very wet. We did all look a bit unearthly, gathered together in our swaithes of blue plastic waiting to be herded on board. It was a lovely, refreshing ride, and when the boat actually went into the centre of the falls, it was one of the most beautiful experiences of the trip. It is almost overpoweringly romantic, standing underneath the full force of nature like that. Mike and I stole a small kiss, just like all the honeymoon couples around us.

Poor Jon was feeling unwell again on the way back, and Jenny went to sit down with him, away from the rail, even though this meant she missed the best view. She insisted that Mike and I stay where we were, to absorb the experience. It was very touching to see her willingness to sacrifice her own pleasure for our sake.

Afterwards we went to a restaurant, but Jon had been sick again on board the 'Maid of the Mist' and was asleep on the back seat of the car. So we stretched him out and I had my lunch brought out to the car park – not the most salubrious of venues but although Jenny offered to stay with Jon again, I felt it was my turn to be unselfish.

7th May

Today we met up with Uncle Jack and Aunty Mave and went to the Niagara Falls, which turned out to be a bit of a con. Mum had built it up to be the experience of a lifetime. She said it was a favourite haunt of honeymoon couples, and so romantic that you 'couldn't fail to be drawn in by its majestic beauty'. Yes, she bought the guide book. Me? I'd prefer somewhere with a bit more life for my honeymoon. After you've looked at the water, what are you supposed to do next? There's not even a night club.

Niagara Falls is actually an awful lot of water crashing down a hillside in full view of a main road, hundreds of sightseers and rows and rows of cars and souvenir shops. I think Niagara also has more than half the world's population of plastic macs. I nearly died when I realized I was expected to wear one. It wouldn't have surprised me to find someone I knew there, to witness my shame and discover what a naff family I have.

There are basically two ways to 'see' the Falls. Actually you can't possibly miss them – they're huge and if you stand at the roadside you get wet. But 'seeing' properly apparently means getting completely drenched by joining a few hundred other people in getting as close to the water as possible. So, you have two choices. The hideous yellow plastic mac company takes you walking under the falls, and the hideous blue plastic mac company takes you out in a rickety boat to sway about a bit at the bottom of them. My mum had set her heart on the boat option.

It's difficult to describe the sight of hundreds of people queuing up in the sun, slightly steaming from being wrapped from head to toe in full length sheets of blue polythene, waiting to get onto a boat which takes all these blue creatures out into the middle of a river and then back. When I realized what we were doing I offered – actually I begged – to be the one to stay behind with Lizzie, who thank God was considered far too little for the trip. But no, Aunty Mave would have none of it. 'I couldn't possibly let you miss out on this,' she said. Gee, thanks.

Next, I tried Jon. Having stuffed himself with sweets and fizzy pop at Aunty Mave and Uncle Jack's yesterday,

85

and having waded through extra maple syrup on his breakfast pancakes, he was very deservedly sick twice in the car on the way. I had to admire his precision, though. 'I feel sick,' he said, then he got out a plastic bag, threw up into it and handed it over to me, natural as a lord of the manor, to hang on to until we could stop. Anyway, he was feeling quite poorly, so I offered to stay with him while Mum and Dad went on this trip of a lifetime, Aunty Mave having her hands full with the baby. But Jon perked up when he saw the boat, so that was that.

Being swathed in blue plastic was bad enough, but Mum was SO EMBARRASSING!!! She kept squealing like a small piglet about how beautiful it was, and fighting through her mac thing to dig out her camera. She must have used a whole film just on shots of water, and the way she takes photos I bet they'll end up looking like someone's bathroom tap. But there was worse to come. She and Dad started getting all moony, and cuddling up to each other. They actually snogged each other, in full view of everyone, right there on the boat. It turned my stomach. Honestly, parents don't understand what it's like to be with them when they behave like that in public.

Fortunately, Jon said he felt sick again, and I was able to get away from Mum and Dad by taking him away from the rail to the centre of the boat where he could sit down. We pretended not to be with them.

As we came back to land, Jon threw up, very neatly again, over the side of the rail in full view of the queue waiting to get on. I bet there were a few second thoughts about the trip then.

We finished off with lunch at a fish and chip restaurant, with Mum and Jon in the car because she was worried about him being sick in there, too. I felt sorry for her then, but it was no more than she deserved for behaving like a teenager on the 'Maid of the Mist'.

We left Toronto at about twelve, and although the flight took five hours, it was only two o'clock when we arrived at Victoria! The time difference thing here is really spooky. From Vancouver, we had to change from a big airliner to a small plane for the last bit of the journey. Victoria is on an island, and the little plane took us across the water. There were only about twenty seats – it was like a toy plane. The view from the window was amazing – loads of little islands glistening in the sun, great-looking beaches everywhere, and Vancouver Island looked so beautiful I even felt a bit excited, though I miss George so much it aches. Jon loved the plane – he thought they might let him fly it on the way back, since it was so little! The flight only lasts twenty-five minutes, but Mum managed to miss the whole thing by falling asleep as soon as she sat down – typical, after all the enthusing she was doing on the way to Toronto about the spectacular views from that plane which turned out to be clouds, clouds, sea and more clouds.

One of the people from Dad's company came to the airport to meet us – he and his wife live just opposite where we're going to be. The car was really neat – huge great white thing, with enough space in the boot for several bodies – ideal for the mass murderer, or for a family of five with enough luggage to create a new town. The stuff we have to lug around for Lizzie is incredible, even though Mum insists she kept it all to a minimum. Still, Mr Troy's car was like a bottomless pit, and swallowed two trolley loads of luggage, Lizzie's pushchair and five passengers without a groan. I hope the car the company have laid on for Dad is like that. I also hope that Mr Troy isn't a mass murderer. He has a very kind face, but he wears a large hat...

The house is brill – much nicer than ours, though I was kind enough to Mum and Dad not to say so. There is a huge cellar, with a TV room, laundry room, bathroom and a bedroom. The ground floor has the kitchen, living room, a study and another bedroom, and finally upstairs is another bathroom and two more bedrooms. The garden has a tree house – explored by Jon within five minutes flat of seeing it. There's a kind of porch on stilts just outside the kitchen door which overlooks the garden. All the houses around here have them – they call it the deck, and as there's a barbecue and chairs and stuff out there I suppose they must eat outside quite a lot.

I decided to have the cellar bedroom, as I'm the oldest – it's like living in a flat, almost. Jon was well choked off, and was all set to cause a fuss. But then I pointed out to him that the cellar was probably really spooky at night, easy to break into from the back garden, and he would be two floors down from Mum and Dad, so no-one would hear him scream. Suddenly he wasn't so interested in the cellar any more...

I will be well away from the rest of the family at night – no-one to nag if I watch telly until the small hours, no-one to complain if the stereo (also in the cellar) is too loud – I think I could get to like it here.

May 8th

I am so tired I don't feel as if I have ever slept, or indeed as if I will ever feel normal again. The time change to Toronto was awful, and Lizzie has only just adapted to that. Now we have another three hour time change so it will start all over again. Even though the flight was uneventful I still felt exhausted by the time we got to Vancouver. Then I saw the plane which would take us out to the Island and, tired as I was, I could easily have got back on the airliner and returned to Toronto. It looked like one of those toys you fly by remote control; it was also old and decrepit-looking. I told Mike it didn't look very safe, and he laughed and said what did I expect?

The pilot arrived just about the same time we did, and he looked rather shifty. The hostess looked nervous to me, as if she knew something about the pilot that we didn't. I decided to keep my fears to myself, since Jenny and Jon and Mike seemed happy enough to dice with death. I clasped my sleeping baby to my bosom, closed my eyes tight and let it all wash over me. Jenny was perversely making comments about how beautiful the view was just to wind me up, I think; I certainly wasn't prepared to look.

Henry Troy, from Mike's work, met us at the airport. The weather is very pleasant – bright, but with a fresh breeze. The Troys have invited us over for tea tomorrow, once we have settled in, and they will fill us in on all the details about the area that we need to know. They live just opposite to us. The house is lovely; bright, spacious and with a big enough garden to keep the children happy. Jenny and Jon were surprisingly amicable about who would sleep where. I thought they might fight over the cellar bedroom, which is almost like a self-contained apartment, but Jon decided he would rather be in the bedroom next to ours, which is rather touching.

The worst is over now. No more long journeys, not much longer until we have all, including Lizzie, adapted to the new time zone and settled into a routine. Mike has a couple of days to 'orientate' as his company calls it, before he has to go into the office and make a start. We are sitting on the porch enjoying a quiet drink while Lizzie dozes (for which we will pay at two a.m., no doubt) before we start unpacking. I expect it will take Jenny as long to unpack her stuff as it will the rest of us put together. If she left anything at all behind in England, it was not for the want of trying. I tried to explain that Canada was not a primitive outpost and would almost certainly have everything she could buy at home. But Jenny was convinced that there would be no 'decent' *shampoo, deodorant, toothpaste, hair gel, moisturiser...the list goes on. She had a small suitcase full of toiletries, and enough lipstick has crossed the Atlantic to last at least until Christmas. She even brought a huge stack of writing paper and envelopes, as she plans to write to George every day and was worried she might not be able to get the right paper (hers has a little heart in the bottom left hand corner) to say what she really means. I think she has inherited a weird streak from her father's side of the family.*

Jon has declared the house 'brill' and Jenny says it's 'all right'. It's difficult to know what's going on with Jenny – she tries hard to stay cool and grown-up, but simmering underneath she may well be the very opposite. I know she misses George, but I'm sure it's a good thing for them to be apart for a while. They're both too young to get serious, and maybe a few months breathing space will give them the chance to see that. Or it will prove to us all that they really are committed to each other.

May 9th

Hello, Canada! I finally feel like I've arrived. Last night we were invited over to the house next door. I thought it would be incredibly boring stuff. But not only did Chas and Miriam (our neighbours) insist that we ate loads of the most amazing ice cream (as well as ply Mum and Dad with cocktails) but they also have the most drop dead gorgeous son I have seen. George is, of course, gorgeous as well. But Dirk next door is so good-looking you feel like he doesn't even belong on this planet. He's about six foot four, and sort of golden brown with white-blond hair in a shaggy heap down to his shoulders. Then there are these truly amazing blue eyes which catch the light and shine out at you, and perfect white teeth.

On top of all that, as if there could possibly be more,

Dirk is a keen hockey player and swimmer. He was wearing a skimpy T-shirt and his body is all muscle and golden glow. Phew! If I wasn't so determined to be true to George I'd be seriously tempted. But with things being the way they are, I have to put his gorgeousness out of my mind, now that I've acknowledged it. He is a couple of years older than me, home for the summer from university in Ottawa, and said he'd be happy to show me around Victoria. He works shifts at the leisure centre as a pool lifeguard and sports coach. Tomorrow he's free after 4 o'clock, and asked me if I wanted to 'go downtown' with him. Apparently a lot of people our age go down to a fish bar overlooking the harbour, where you can do a bit of rollerbooting, drink Coke and generally chill out. Dirk says 'chill out' a lot, but it doesn't sound at all naff in his accent, the way it does back home.

I did of course make sure that George got into the conversation early on, so that Dirk wouldn't get the wrong idea. I told him quite clearly that it would be good to get to know a few people BECAUSE I would be very lonely without my boyfriend. Dirk nodded and gave this slow, knees to water smile. He said he hoped I wouldn't miss George too much to have a good time. I could scarcely breathe. If I wasn't 100 per cent committed to George (who is probably having a good time without me anyway) this boy could be very, very, dangerous.

9th May

We have settled in very nicely, and are beginning to get our bearings. We have toured Victoria, and found it to be a very beautiful and friendly city. Jon loves the school he is going to, just three or four minutes drive away. I thought its size would be intimidating after his own small primary, but he loves it – and the other kids love him, too. He keeps us informed on all

91

the Canadian sports news, and is becoming a big fan of baseball. The other children have adopted him as a class mascot for the four weeks he will be with them, I gather.

The neighbours have also been very welcoming, and I hope the people staying in our house are receiving even half the kindness we are experiencing here. We have been loaned maps, field glasses and beautiful picture books of the area, and have the telephone number of everyone we could possibly need to contact for anything at all. We also have our neighbours' phone numbers. Even though they are only fifty yards or so away, everyone here seems to telephone rather than come over!

The other evening we were invited for drinks with Chas and Miriam next door. They are charming, and their son Dirk looks as though he has travelled from Mount Olympus for a short season of slumming with the lesser mortals (thanks in large part, I suspect, to many hours in gyms, at hairdressers and under sun beds!). Jenny's eyes nearly popped out of her head, and I almost had to ask her to put her tongue back in her mouth. Poor George. I'm not sure any memory of him crossed her brain during the first hour. Dirk offered to take Jenny out and she said yes so fast I was embarrassed. Then she recovered her cool a bit and mentioned that she had a sort of boyfriend (hear that George? Sort of boyfriend) back in England, and so she hadn't been doing much socialising lately. The two of them then exchanged a look which had all the adults politely looking away!

Dirk is at university and seems very mature for Jenny, although he is only nineteen. He came round for her last night and they went to his usual haunt down in the city centre. Jenny crawled back in at well after midnight, and said she had had an O.K. time. She was suspiciously casual and nonchalant about the whole thing. Dirk is coming by later today to take her to meet some more of his friends. I feel very uneasy about this. Jenny insists that this is just someone she can spend time with (or 'chill out' as she puts it) to show her around during this first month when she has to study and Jon's at school so we can't go anywhere much. I was the one who thought it would be good for Jenny to spread her wings and not get too tied down with George, and she was very quick to point that out. But that was before I thought Jenny might throw herself so wholeheartedly into spreading her wings at the earliest opportunity.

Dirk is very charming, but he's rather smooth and sophisticated for Jenny. He does not give the impression of being a deep thinker. I think he finds the idea of an English girl eyeing him up quite amusing. He knows she likes him, and he sort of struts when she's around. I can easily imagine him playing her along for a while and dropping her when he gets bored. It's only a first impression and it's not fair to talk to Jenny about it too much. I did say, casually, that I hoped she wouldn't get too involved. She gave me The Look.

'We're just going to be friends,' she said. 'You know, like me and Sadie. Just because he's a boy, off you go...you're so sexist, Mum'. Hmm. She may be right. On the other hand, I don't remember the last time she spent two hours in the bathroom getting ready to 'chill out' with Sadie...

May 19th

I feel as though I have been here for ages, and I am really at home. Dirk has taught me so much about the history of the place, and introduced me to so many friends, that I feel accepted as one of the group. My accent is different, but otherwise all Dirk's friends feel like old friends of mine, too. It has worked out very well. While

Dirk goes to his job, I study for my 'A' levels. Not even Mum can complain about the amount of work I am putting in there. Then Dirk comes round, and we go to see his friends or just do something relaxing.

Yesterday we played tennis and Dirk was helping me improve my grip. I could feel his breath on the back of my neck as he stood behind me and put his hand over mine to swing the racket. He was so close it made me go all shivery – I haven't even felt that way with George lately. It was like an electric charge. I could almost feel his lips brush my neck, but nothing happened. I'm ashamed to say I was disappointed.

I think he knew the effect being so close has on me, though. He smiled that smile and got really close when we said goodbye. My knees went all funny. How can I be feeling like this about someone I hardly know, with George pining away for me back in England? It feels awful, but I can't stop it feeling good as well. Perhaps Cathy talked a lot of sense after all. What harm could a little scene with Dirk do, as long as George isn't hurt by it?

21st May

I got a really long letter from George today. He said my last two letters had been so short I might as well have sent a postcard. I will telephone him tonight and talk for a long time. I've also written a very long letter, full of kisses and 'I love you's. The problem is, what with writing every other day you sort of run out of things to tell each other about. He's got his brother and sisters, and they're always up to something. George is very witty when he tells me their latest exploits. I can't do things that well. Besides, I'm not doing very much, apart from hanging out with Dirk. It's totally innocent, but I don't want to tell George about him because he might get the wrong idea and think I fancy him. Well of course I DO fancy him, but not that way. I love George, I really do. He's just so far away, and Dirk is so NEAR!

Lizzie has discovered crawling in a very big way over the last couple of weeks. She is driving us mad. Yesterday I found her in the kitchen by the dry goods cupboard. Mum had only popped out to the deck to hang the washing, but Lizzie had managed to empty a bag of tea and a bag of flour on the floor, and was making pretty patterns in it with her fingers. We keep telling Lizzie not to open cupboards, but she just laughs. Mum has no discipline over her at all; she'll end up a spoilt brat, just like Jon.

Talking of Jon, he is really getting on my nerves. I can't wait for his school to finish. He is constantly talking about baseball, and swings and strikes and teams with really weird names that I can't even pronounce. He uses Canadian words as well. He asks Dad to put things in the trunk of the car, stays on the sidewalk when he goes to school and earnestly asks about movies on TV and whether we can buy certain things at the store. Yuk. He even offers to 'take out the trash' just so he can say the words. What a little poser. Me, I stick to my own language and remain truly, patriotically, British.

2nd June

I have been in Canada for one month now. Only three more to go, and then George and I will never, ever, be parted again. I spoke to him last night, and he sounded all sort of lost and lonely. A letter from Sadie came this morning – she's coming out to stay with us in August! It will be so great – she says there's lots going on at school and all over the place that I need to be filled in on. She'll be staying for two weeks. Cathy was hoping to come as well, but it looks like she won't be able to get the time off work. Sadie says she doesn't think Ted will be around for much longer, but she doesn't say why.

I have been working very hard on the Biology coursework tasks I was given to do while I was off school. It's so hard to get going when you have no-one else to ask questions or chat to. Roll on the end of the month. Mum says if I work hard now we'll start to treat our remaining time as a 'cultural and educational experience rather than a mere book-learning one'. What this means is she's going to give up nagging me about studies and we're going to party!

Dirk has been doing double shifts the last couple of days and we haven't seen each other much. Last night he came over too late to go out anywhere, so we sat out on the deck drinking coke and comparing countries – we had a good laugh.

The idea that we speak the same language is a bit of a myth, and a well travelled teenager needs to know her way around. For instance, the public loos are called washrooms. This implies that you can take your dirty laundry with you, but you'd look pretty silly struggling through the doorway loaded with a week's worth of knickers to be confronted by a line of loos and some very small washbasins. In private homes the loo is called a bathroom. Most bathrooms don't have a bath, which can be very confusing when you think about it.

Canadians spend a lot of time eating and drinking. They have restaurants for everything – there are even restaurants only serving doughnuts! We eat out quite a lot. Mum says there's no point in cooking when you have so much choice for so little money. You can't travel more than a mile without coming across 'Hal's Happy Eating Joint' or 'Family Fast Food'. Fast means fast here, too. Yesterday we ordered four dinners at a McDonald's and it was on the tray before Mum even began to search through her purse for the right money. Mum, being a bit old for this sort of thing, gets rather confused by the money. Every time we pay for something, she goes through the same ritual – the hunt through the purse, then the pockets, then the hopeless smile at the assistant and an outstretched hand. The assistant smiles, takes the right money and sometimes gives us a quick lesson in which coin is which. Mum, knowing that she will forget everything the assistant is telling her within two minutes of leaving the till, says how grateful she is. It is so embarrassing. But not as embarrassing, mind you, as her attempts to 'blend in with the local community'. She's even bought this hideous hat – complete with elastic under-chin strap, of course – which I am trying to 'lose' for her as a favour to mankind.

June 4th

Jenny and Jon's eyes were like saucers when they saw the size of some of the shopping malls around here. It's becoming one of our main sources of entertainment during the day, while Mike is at work. I am beginning to get the hang of the money and I'm quite proud of the way I've coped so far, although the tax still confuses me a bit. We have gone around the local supermarket a few times now, and I'm beginning to feel quite at home in a different sort of culture, especially now that I have a straw hat from the local market.

5th June

I am never going to get all this work finished. I've got stacks of Biology still left to do, and three History essays for which I haven't even got the right books. Then I'm supposed to read a whole book of Sylvia Plath poems (she's a real downer for bedtime reading) and complete a major assignment in English for when I get back. At this rate I'll see nothing of Canada except the walls of this house.

Dirk is away for two weeks now, off to Toronto with his friends. So I've got no-one to talk to. Mum spends all her time with Lizzie and Jon, and Dad is so grumpy these days I'm not keen to talk to him either. I think he's beginning to feel this trip wasn't such a good idea after all. To cap it all, George has missed two letters. I should have had one today and one the day before yesterday, but there's been nothing. I called him at home but there was no answer. I hope he's O.K. If he's out with another girl I will kill him.

I told Mum how fed up I was when she brought me a sandwich at lunchtime, and she promptly decided that I should have a break, go shopping with her and then get back to the work this evening. Great! Shopping all afternoon with my aged mother and baby sister and a fun-filled evening drawing diagrams of a piece of bread and butter travelling on its merry way through the human digestive system. What more could a girl ask from life?

June 6th

Mike is beginning to feel the pressure at work a bit now. It has not been as straightforward a job as he had hoped, and the problem is the system is so new that there's no-one he can really talk to about it. He's basically the one who's supposed to be giving everyone else the advice. I think he got a very high billing and feels desperate to live up to the reputation that went before him. He looks so tired when he comes home, which is usually very late. He doesn't see much of Lizzie these days, and even Jon is in bed quite often when he gets back. I didn't envisage our trip of a lifetime being quite like this, but I'm not complaining. Once Jon finishes school we'll be able to get out and about a lot more, and hopefully Mike's teething troubles at work will have sorted themselves out by then and he'll be able to join us sometimes.

Jenny has been working very hard at her studies, and maybe even a bit too hard. She has been grumpy the last couple of days. I took her shopping this afternoon as a treat to lighten her mood.

June 7th

One miserable letter from George today, which hardly said anything. I have written three long letters full of interesting details about my life here since I last heard from him, and he sends me little more than a postcard which tells me he's working hard and missing me. I'm sure he's up to something. We spoke on the phone last night (and that's another thing. I'm always the one doing the phoning. I know we agreed to do it that way because it's much cheaper to call from Canada than it is to call to England, but if he really loved me he wouldn't be able to resist calling just now and then would he?). I asked him if he had been to the youth centre and he said no, but he answered a bit quickly. Guilt? If Louise Ann Maynard has moved in on him I will never forgive her. Or him, the stupid idiot.

8th June

There is a real atmosphere developing in the house. Mike is snapping at everyone, Jenny is being impossible about everything and Lizzie is intent on taking the place apart piece by piece. As soon as I take my eyes off her she's racing off to do some more mischief. If only we had a playpen – or Jenny wasn't so miserable that she could amuse her in the garden for a while. The only cheerful one in the family right now is Jon, who loves it at his Canadian school and is beginning to talk like a native, as well as supporting the school baseball team with all the fervour of a devoted fan.

I don't think Jenny is doing very much work. She sits down in her room for hours on end, and won't do anything for me except grudgingly, and with a huge sigh that makes my heart sink whenever I need to ask. She is also complaining non-stop about everything Canadian. She doesn't like the shops, she doesn't like the food, the cinemas are showing rubbish films, the magazines talk about film stars she's never heard of, the clothes are naff, people who smile at her in shops are getting on her nerves, the television is boring...it goes on and on and on, a constant whingeing drone. She and Mike had a big row this evening when he tried to make a real effort to plan something for us to do at the weekend as a family. He desperately needs to unwind, and I suggested going up the island to see the rain forests. No, Jenny didn't want to look at a load of old trees. A day by the ocean? The sea is too cold. A boat trip out to the little islands she had liked the look of? Too much hassle.

Mike asked her what she wanted to do, and she said 'Go home'. That was it. I could see her winding him up throughout the conversation, and at that point he snapped and said he would plan something he and I wanted to do, and the children could lump it or stay behind.

Jon got very pompous and said he hadn't said he wanted to go home, and Mike told him to shut up. Lizzie started to cry, Jenny ran down to her room slamming three doors in the process, and another quiet family meal ended in tatters.

We can't go on like this. Jenny's foul mood and Mike's tension at work are dragging us all down. Mike can't help the pressure at work, and Jenny I suppose is missing George and her friends. But she could at least make an effort to enjoy the country now she's here, and she doesn't seem prepared to. I'm going to *have to think of something to put a stop to all this, or the trip will be ruined for everyone.*

Dad is being so unreasonable. He can't hack it at work so he takes it out on us at home. Last night he started going on about how he needed a break at the weekend, and gave us all these really naff ideas for outings. Well if he didn't want my opinion why did he ask for it? I told him what I thought of his ideas and he just went bananas. It's not my fault they made me come here and it's not my fault I don't like it. I want to be back home with George and Sadie and all my friends. I want to be at school (yes, heaven help me, even with Jack J. Jackson!) doing work at the same pace as everyone else and forgetting to give in homework. Instead I'm stuck in this foreign country where everyone smiles all the time and pretends everything's perfect. It hasn't even rained. I just want to go home.

Jon will finish school soon, and I've got all the tourist leaflets out to make an itinerary for the rest of our stay. We are going to travel around the Island for a few days, taking in a boat trip to see if we can spot some whales. We're also going to visit the rain forests, and take the ferry over to Vancouver to see the sights, and dozens of other things. We might even be able to hire a camper van for the last few days, if Mike finishes on time. Jon and I are quite excited. Jenny is still in this awful mood she's decided to adopt. But tonight I told her that we would be sending her home on the first available flight if she doesn't lighten up. It will be worth stretching the credit card bill and paying for it for months after we get back, if it stops the weight of her whingeing at me all the time. It was a mistake to bring her, I can see that now. She's too inflexible to cope without her own home and her own friends. I would have worried about leaving her at home, but anything would have been better than this.

12th June

Mum and Dad have decided to send me home! Mum said they had worked out that their credit card would just about cover the air fare, and that they would try and get me on a flight in a couple of days time. I thought she was just saying it at first, but then she pulled out the dates and flight times available. Isn't that just typical of parents? I mean, if it was all right for me to be at home why couldn't they just leave me there in the first place? Now they've decided they don't want me hanging around and they're going to send me all that way, on my own, because they think I'm going to spoil their precious holiday. Just as we were revving up to the interesting bit as well, all the beaches and travelling around and having a good time instead of being stuck in Saanich.

I have been a bit miserable lately, but it's mostly to do with George being so vague when I talk to him on the phone and his letters being so short. I miss him so much. But I want to have this holiday as well. I don't want to be packed off home and then hear about all the great things they've done when they come back. And I especially don't want Gran looking after me, not even if it means I can see George. And I would really miss Mum and Dad and Jon – and Lizzie would be a different child by the time they came home.

I can't believe Mum is seriously thinking about sending me back, but she is. I've got to 'shape up and stop being being such a little misery', or they're going to parcel me back. Sadie will kill me if she misses her trip to Canada. It took her for ever to persuade her parents to let her come, and she's working every weekend as well as doing a paper round to pay for it.

I can see that for the good of everyone I will have to put my own heartache aside and pretend to be enjoying myself. At least some of the things they have planned sound O.K. I will take loads of photos so that George can share the experiences with me. I will have to draw on all my inner strength, and make the best of my time here. At least there's Dirk – he's really good fun to be with.

15th June

Jenny is a lot more cheerful and is making a real effort to get involved with our plans, now that she understands wallowing in self-pity isn't going to get her anywhere. She even volunteered to take Jon and Lizzie out to the playground while I caught up on some laundry and household chores. I think she is actually quite excited about some of the trips we've planned, but she doesn't want to appear un-cool or look as if she's given in. I could tell she was very shocked that we were prepared to send her home. I wish I had thought of it before, perhaps all this nonsense would have ended sooner. But at least we can start to enjoy ourselves properly now.

Mike came home a lot more cheerful last night, too. They have managed to resolve the problems they had in the early stages of the work, and things look as though they could be back on schedule in a week or two. He will still have to put in some very long hours until then but he has obviously achieved something important and he is the old enthusiastic computer boffin again rather than the haggard executive who's been coming home lately.

Dirk has been off the scene for a while, but

103

tomorrow he is coming out with us for the day to show us a good place to swim. I think Jenny is risking making a fool of herself here. I've seen Dirk's type before. I think he's just a bit too smoothly charming. He sees Jenny as someone to have a good time with, but he'll take what he can and then run a mile if she starts to get serious. I hope she's got more sense.

George's letters are a bit sporadic, although Jenny still writes almost every day, perhaps because she feels guilty. Does George know about Dirk, I wonder? I suspect not, which leads me also to wonder how Jenny is going to keep it quiet when we get back to England. Has she realized that Jon is bound to mention Dirk – especially if she tells him not to? It could be quite entertaining.

16th June

Dirk is back from Toronto, and today he took us all (except Dad) out to a place called Sooke. It's a place where there used to be a volcano, and there are these volcanic pot holes in a deep forest. The river runs down a mountain through woodland, and every now and then there are small, very deep lakes. You can jump off high rocks into them and still never reach the bottom. Dirk reckons they are at least a hundred feet deep in places.

We had an amazing day. The weather was hot and the water was lovely. Dirk met a couple of friends there (he seems to know EVERYONE!) and we left Mum and Lizzie and Jon sitting on a little beach paddling away and we went upstream to some very high rocks. The top of one of them was seventy feet above the water, and Dirk and his friends climbed up and just jumped off! I was scared stiff just watching them, no way could I jump in too. But it didn't matter – just looking at Dirk was compensation enough. He has the most perfect body I've seen on anyone, even in pictures. And he's so fit. He climbs these rocks as if he were walking on an ordinary road.

Afterwards I did jump from some rocks, further down where they weren't so high. You go deep, deep down into the water and it seems like ages before you reach the surface again, but it's lovely. Dirk pulled me out of the water, and for a moment our bodies sort of brushed together. I don't know if he even noticed, but I'm ashamed to say I really wanted him to. I feel confused about the whole thing. I miss George so much, but a whole summer without any kind of relationship at all with anybody is going to be so hard...

I hope we can go to Sooke again – Dad would love it. The only downer of the day was the loo. It's a glorified bucket in a hut, and the stench is almost unbearable. I survived by going into the forest, but Mum can't cope so well with primitive conditions and spent all afternoon with her legs crossed!

16th June

We had a beautiful day out at Sooke Pot Holes. Dirk drove us there in his father's car; we would not have found it on our own. It's a beautiful place, full of huge trees and bubbling clean water and volcanic holes which are crisp and clean and lovely to swim in. Dirk and Jenny played with the little ones while I went for a swim and then they struck out on their own. Jenny and Dirk look very good together, and they get on like a house on fire. This has the makings of a true holiday romance, and I'm curious to see how Jenny copes with it. There is definitely something about Dirk which puts me on edge, but maybe that's purely sympathy for poor old George.

I was sorry Mike couldn't come with us, but at least he's happy at work now. We decided to go back again soon.

I have kissed Dirk. Dirk has kissed me. Which way round was it exactly? I don't know, I just know that I feel so guilty about George the ground will surely open up and swallow me whole any minute. I didn't mean to do it. We were joking around at the harbour, and I was taking the mickey out of all these unheard of rock bands Dirk likes. He said he had a spare ticket to a really good concert which would educate me thoroughly into the superiority of the Canadian bands' sound, and if I was nice to him he would let me have it. I said what did he mean, nice, and he said he meant a kiss.

I meant to give him a quick peck on the cheek, honestly I did. But my lips sort of missed and met his mouth instead. And it was a bit longer than a quick kiss should be, too. A lot longer, actually. I couldn't seem to stop it. I tried thinking of George, but the awful thing was, at that moment I couldn't even remember what he looked like. So I thought I might as well enjoy the experience. Dirk is a brilliant kisser. George is good, but Dirk is more experienced.

Dirk was interested in a bit more than kissing, I think, but I managed to pull away. I didn't say anything, because I don't want him to think I'm a prude or a little kid, but I think he got the message. I love George, Dirk knows that. But there's nothing wrong in kissing as long as we're both clear where we stand, is there? After all, how do you get to be a good kisser without practising different styles on different people? And I do want to be a good kisser – for George.

Afterwards we walked hand in hand round the harbour, with all the little boats twinkling their lights and the hotel lit up against the sky. It was very romantic. When he kissed me again, I did remind Dirk that I had a boyfriend at home. He shrugged. 'Let's just have a good time while you're here.' That's what he said. I think that's an excellent idea. No strings, no tears, just a good time and someone to fill the gap while I'm missing George so much. So why do I feel guilty?

Dirk and Jenny went out on their own yesterday evening, instead of with the usual little bunch of friends. Jenny came back looking just a touch furtive. I asked her if she had a good time and she said yes. Then the shutter came down. You can tell exactly when Jenny is not willing to talk. Instead of a frame by frame account of every last detail of her evening, she confines herself to the shortest possible answer and then changes the subject. She must have been desperate to avoid this one, as she even started clearing the draining board and asked me if I would like a cup of tea! I wish I knew where all this was headed. I hope Jenny understands how far away England is from Canada, and how much she'll lose if she threatens her relationship with George for what could be a no-hoper with Dirk. Not that I will say that to Jenny. I'm sensible enough to know that a mother's advice is the kiss of death to any teenager.

We went into Victoria for the whole day today. Mum was determined to bore us in the name of education, so we went first to the museum. As museums go, it's actually quite nifty, but I didn't tell Mum that. The trick is to make her think you're bored out of your socks but determined not to show it. Then she feels guilty about dragging you along, and spends money on you. I have practised this to a fine art, but Jon is a bit young to understand yet. He dived at the displays with far too much enthusiasm. It was due to my efforts alone that we abandoned the idea of a packed lunch (miserable little triangles of egg and cress) and went to a McDonalds instead.

Inside the museum were loads of exhibits telling the history of Canada – more interesting than some of the European rubbish I have to plough through for 'A' level. They had an actual old ship you could go inside, and an ancient street of shops. One of the best bits was the prehistoric display, complete with life sized hairy mammoth and sabre-toothed tiger. They only had a waist-high barrier. So there was no-one around at all when I lifted Jon over the barrier and took a photo of him shaking the mammoth's trunk and saying 'How do you do?'. I took one of him sitting on the tiger too, but we had to be quick so I'm not sure how well it will come out. I was amazed there were no alarms or anything when I hoicked him over the rail. If I'd known I'd have gone over myself, but I didn't risk it. An enraged attendant is much more likely to believe that a seven-year-old acted in exuberant ignorance of the rules than someone my age. You would think they'd take better care of their precious inheritance, wouldn't you? I mean, I don't suppose Canadians are any more law-abiding and careful than the Brits, are they?

In fact, Victoria is sometimes called Little England around here. Loads of British people settled here over the years. There is an 'English' pub (complete with sawdust on the floor; I'm not sure the owner has been in Britain recently) and references to Queen Elizabeth all over the place. You can even go for a ride on a red London double decker bus, which takes you touring around Victoria. There were crowds of people waiting to get on, and many admiring passers-by. Mum said she had travelled to school on one every day of her school life, and she just couldn't see their charm.

In the afternoon we went to this undersea kingdom. Mum waited outside with Lizzie, as Mum is too squeamish to cope with anything which has rubbery skin and teeth! It was neat. Sharks and eels and lobsters just sail past your nose behind these huge glass screens. The gift shop was excellent, and I managed to buy some great presents to take back. Jon insisted on buying a giant inflatable plastic killer whale and trying to blow it up in the street, complete with amazing sound effects which were embarrassing. In the end I managed to persuade him that it would blow away and it was much safer to keep it in his duffle bag.

Dad met us later and we went to ye olde English tea shoppe for dinner. I think this place is one of the weirdest I've been to here. It looks exactly like a tea shop in an old-fashioned story book – white lacy cloths on the tables, china teapots, waitresses in long black dresses with crisp white frilly aprons – the works. On the wall there's a huge portrait of Prince Charles and Diana looking radiantly happy on their wedding day. Has anyone told them yet? In another corner Princess Anne gazes deep into the eyes of Captain Mark Phillips, whom she split up with when I was a baby. Dad says it's strange that everyone knows who Mark Phillips is, but no-one can tell you the name of Anne's current husband. He's right, too. I tried it on the neighbours when we got home.

Jon ordered roast beef and Yorkshire pudding, as he misses his Sunday dinner. But when they brought it, it was smothered in thick (instant?) gravy and he couldn't eat it. Dad was really mean about it. He scraped the gravy off rather than sending it back and expected Jon to eat it. But the meat was soaked in the foul liquid. I wouldn't have eaten it, and I said so. Dad and I had a row, in that very particular hushed whisper you have to adopt in a public place. Poor Jon just stared mournfully at his meat and picked warily at the bits of Yorkshire pudding that the gravy had missed. When the waitress came and asked if everything was all right Dad said yes and Jon said no at the same time. Mum did her helpless foreigner bit and explained that we had not expected the gravy. The waitress looked surprised and said she thought there was always gravy with roast meat, but she laughed and said she could tell from our accents that we were the experts. They gave Jon two buttered crumpets instead, and didn't charge for them, which was nice. I don't know why Mum and Dad have to make such a big deal out of these things. You can't take them anywhere.

July 2nd

We had a rare family outing yesterday, with something to please everyone. We went into Victoria, and started with the museum. Jon was very intrigued by the hairy mammoth and wouldn't move away from it, so Jenny very sweetly agreed to keep an eye on him while I wheeled Lizzie around the ecology section. Jenny hates museums, so this was a particularly kind act. She didn't complain once the whole time we were there, although you could tell she was just trying to look as though she was having a good time so as not to spoil it for Jon and me.

McDonalds is much more Jenny's scene, and so we went there for lunch (Jon had happily munched his way through most of my beautifully cut English sandwiches anyway by then). Jon and Jenny went into the Undersea World to ooh and aah over vicious creatures of the deep (and green turtles, which you could touch, apparently). I stayed outside with Lizzie, partly because I don't think she would have endured being wheeled around in semi-darkness with no idea what was going on, but partly, I have to confess, because of Jon. He is very interested in the eating habits of animals. He is an expert on how crocodiles roll their victims to disorientate them, and the various ways animals can paralyse their prey before tucking in (sometimes before the creature is dead). He likes to share his new-found knowledge, and frankly I don't have a strong enough stomach for it.

110

Jon came out raving about the sharks' teeth and evil little eyes, and Jenny had a bulging gift shop bag. I'm not sure she would have been able to describe a single sea creature, but she knew the layout of the gift shop intimately. Jon bought an inflatable killer whale as a momento of his trip. It's rather large, and I hope he doesn't try to inflate it on the plane when we go home.

I had hardly hoped that Mike would be able to meet us at the harbour as agreed if he could get away early, but there he was. We went to the Rose Tea Garden for dinner. It is a beautiful period restaurant, small but friendly, which has perfectly captured the feel of traditional England. The children were embarrassing, as usual, with their comments about the decor and the food, but we have grown to expect that from our children and we have learned to accept that you can't take them anywhere without being humiliated. It was good to be out as an entire family. I suppose this will be the last family holiday we have. Jenny will no doubt be planning her future holidays with friends and eventually her own family, and our holidays will only be memories. So it seemed most appropriate that we spend some time in this little time warp of a restaurant.

5th July

Today Dirk didn't have to work, so he offered to take us to a really neat beach. When we reached the beach a mist had rolled in off the ocean and you could hardly see a thing. It was also very cold. I thought that would be an end of the swim, sun and picnic that we had planned, but Dirk is clearly some sort of boy scout. He looked around to get the feel of the weather and simply opened the boot of his dad's car and hey presto! Two woolly rugs and some firelighters. He then set Jon to work looking

111

for wood. There is so much logging here that wood just rolls out of the sea all the time, and trees go right down to the beach in most of the places we've seen. There are no bars, snack booths or even proper paths in places – just the ocean, long stretches of beach and the forest behind it. And we mustn't forget Mum's particular favourite tourist attraction, the forest station loo, alias a bottomless bucket suspended over an open trench. I managed to get a picture of Mum's face as she approached it.

Dotted here and there at the top of the beach there were big metal bowls sunk into the ground, with grilles over the top. Dirk explained that these were camp fire sites. He seemed surprised that we don't have them in England – it's very common over here to set up a camp on the beach and barbecue your dinner. I hope he gets to visit England some day. I can't wait to see his face when he claps eyes on Blackpool or Bognor Regis!

Jon and Dirk made themselves busy doing the hunter gatherer thing while Mum snuggled up under a blanket with Lizzie and I strained my eyes trying to see past the shoreline through this thick, cold mist. I didn't believe it would ever lift, and couldn't see the point of staying, but Dirk called me a person of little faith and kissed me, smack on the lips, in full view of Mum! Luckily she didn't see – even more luckily, nor did Jon. I told Dirk not to do that again, and he laughed and said I'd gone all red.

Dirk got a lovely camp fire going and we had lunch sharing its warmth. He was right though – soon after lunch the mist lifted and you could actually see the coastline of the United States of America! Plus there were these lovely little rocky islands that you could walk out to once the tide went out a bit. It was amazing. We all had a lovely day, and it was thanks to Dirk. He's great company. I feel guilty about George every time I say that.

Dirk packed us all up in his father's car and took us to the coast today. We had a lovely time, and I felt sorry for poor old Mike who had to spend all day and half the evening in the office. The beach we went to was very rugged and remote-looking, not at all the children's kind of thing usually. You couldn't even buy an ice cream. But the scenery more than made up for that.

Dirk was in his element, showing off his skills right at the start by rustling up a camp fire when the mist came down. But he was very good with Jon, involving him in gathering the wood for a fire and answering all Jon's questions about the weather, and what you'd be able to see if you could see anything. (The USA is clearly visible on a good day, as we discovered.) Jenny sat looking out to sea in a carefully practised, romantic sort of way (I'm not sure if Dirk noticed) and Lizzie and I played the role of the womenfolk, huddled together under Dirk's protective woollen rug. I think he expected that, and it seemed the least we could do to assist in the macho image he was after.

My first impression has not changed. Dirk is a poser and I felt quite irritated with him today. This is unfair when he has been so considerate about taking us out. But I don't trust him. He kissed Jenny, not in a brotherly way, right under my nose as though she were already his property. I pretended not to see, and was glad to hear Jenny hiss something at him which I hope was an instruction to lay off. I wish I knew what was going on with those two. Whenever I hear a snatch of Jenny talking to George it's all the usual lovey-dovey missing-you-dreadfully stuff, and it's not right that she should keep stringing George along if things are developing with Dirk. If she's not careful, she's going to end up with a double dose of hurt. George is a gentle and generous soul, but as he proved with that girl at Jenny's school, he's not totally averse to the idea of finding someone else. And I'm pretty sure that after the summer Dirk is not going to want to know some English schoolgirl he killed time with while his university friends were unavailable.

9th July

We seem to have been here, there and everywhere over the last few days – cinema, beaches, museums, shops and more shops, art galleries. Interestingly enough, Mum always manages to get us to the beach or into the forests for an hour or two at the start of the day and then we move on into the town or to somewhere with more 'civilisation' as she calls it. What is actually happening is that she can't face spending a whole day without a nice clean toilet block complete with soap, towels and a flushing loo. She would never admit that, of course, because she hates to think that she is such a wimp that she can't tough it out in the old rugged country, but I know my mum.

Dirk has come out with a us a few times, but I don't think he finds Mum's view of a good time quite up his street. He's more the outdoors sporty type than a culture freak. Like me. But if we keep Mum happy she stops prying into my so-called love life. I am both excited and ashamed to say that things between me and Dirk are becoming more of a holiday romance than just good friends. It's exactly the kind of thing George and I talked about, and so I know he wouldn't mind, but it still feels a bit disloyal. When Dirk kisses me it just sort of melts through any resistance I try. He understands about George and we both know things can't really go anywhere, but sometimes I just sort of wish they could.

I have managed to cool things down a bit between Dirk and Jenny by planning outings that he doesn't have much interest in. It sounds mean, but I don't want him hanging around Jenny too much. On the one hand she's old enough to know what she's doing, I suppose, but on the other I'm convinced she and Dirk are seeing their relationship very differently. She's very attracted to Dirk, and would maybe even let go of George for him. But when they're together, he is so patronising towards her, as though she's a kid and he's the real man of the world. She can't see it, but even Mike, not known for his powers of observation in these matters, commented the other day that Dirk seems to have Jenny dangling on a string. I tried to talk to Jenny about this. I said I thought Dirk was probably going to be a real womanizer one day, and to be careful not to lose her heart. She gave me a withering look and said I had been reading too many trashy novels. Isn't that supposed to be the mother's line? I should have quit then, while I was ahead, but I couldn't resist saying that I thought Dirk had more in mind than a mere innocent holiday romance. The way he looks at her is becoming positively lecherous.

Jenny hit the roof. She accused me – well actually, all 'old people' – of having a filthy and suspicious mind. She said she and George had an understanding, and if she and Dirk liked each other's company that was no-one's business but theirs. I asked her how much George knew about this so-called friendship and she wouldn't answer. I ended my catalogue of blunders with a suggestion that she should at least seek some advice about contraception if she hadn't already done so. I thought I was being very modern and responsible, accepting that she was seventeen and old enough to make decisions for

115

herself. She went completely bananas then, and yelled that I had to stop treating her like a stupid kid! The door slammed so hard I expected it to fall off. Whoops! I knew I should have stayed silent. But when it's your own daughter, and when she is so clearly on course for disaster, what mother can stop herself at least trying to throw out a life jacket?

13th July

Thank goodness Dad had the day off today and came out with us. Things were bad enough between me and Mum after our row, when I told her to stop interfering in my life. She makes Dirk out to be some kind of sex mad freak, and even implied I might go along with anything he wanted to do, despite the fact that she knows how I feel about George.

Anyway, things have been a bit strained. Then this morning, with brill timing, the photos of the trip to the museum arrived. My illustrious mother got her undies into a right twist when Jon showed her the photos of him, the hairy mammoth and the sabre-toothed tiger, and the one showing her stepping gingerly into the forest loo with the most disgusted, nose-holding expression on her face! We had the pictures developed yesterday. I told Jon not to show the olds those particular ones, but he was so proud of them he couldn't stop himself. They are fine photos.

Dad could see the funny side of it, but Mum did a full scale War Dance of Righteousness. Guest in this country, irresponsible idiot, bad example to a little one etc etc etc. As if Jon needed any encouragement. He's far worse than I ever was at his age, and it has nothing to do with example.

Mum was stiff with rage all morning, and she and Dad had a bit of a bust up about something too, but by lunchtime she was lightening up a bit. We went into the

116

hills above Victoria and walked around on the coastal path. It was good fun.

13th July

Trust Jenny to spoil one of the very few days we can spend with Mike. We had a film developed and some of the shots she has taken are really stupid. It was bad enough to know that she has been sneaking pictures of me in embarrassing moments behind my back, but when I saw the ones where she had incited Jon to climb over the rails at the city museum and maul the exhibits just for a cheap shot, I was mortified. Did I completely waste my time all those years, teaching my children manners and consideration for the environment and other people? What on earth would native Canadians have thought of them if they'd been seen climbing about all over the natural history exhibits? Jenny seems to think that since they weren't seen, it doesn't matter. But what kind of example is that to set a child?

Even Mike laughed when he saw the pictures, which are of Jon and a hairy mammoth and a sabre-toothed tiger. He did not exactly present a united front with me on this. I tried to point out to him that this was very wrong; he just told me to chill out. Where DOES this extraordinary expression come from? What is it supposed to mean? Perhaps we have been away from home for too long.

This situation with Jenny and Dirk colours everything between Jenny and me. I know I over-reacted to the pictures a bit because of all the other things going on between us. But I despair of her ever growing up, I really do.

I am hopping mad. I just telephoned George – usual chat, lots of kissy-kissy missing you stuff. Then I called Sadie, and she said George had shown up at the end of term dance with Jasmine Patel! Of course, he hadn't mentioned this little fact to me three minutes earlier. Sadie hadn't seen them kissing or anything, but they were laughing together and danced even in the smoochy ones, she said.

I wasn't going to call George again, but I couldn't help it. I just got so simmering mad. So at three o'clock in the morning (five o'clock afternoon, his time) I gave him a real ear full. How dare he just go off with someone like that! He said it didn't mean anything, he was just asked by Jasmine if he would go with her because she didn't have anyone to go with. He also said he was getting very lonely and there was no harm in having a friend or two to go out with while I was away. So there's more than one, is there? How about that for undying love and loyalty? I called Sadie straight away to check this out. She said she didn't know of anyone else. And it certainly wasn't Louise Ann Maynard, because she seems to have a thing going with – wait for it – Jack J. Jackson! Sadie has promised to give me all the goss when she arrives, which is only a couple of weeks away, but at the moment it's only a suspicion which she and Sam and Adam are checking out.

George and I didn't part on very good terms, and I'll have to call him again tonight. Mum is not being very sympathetic, either. She said I deserve to be messed around, since I'm doing exactly the same thing. I suppose she means Dirk – well, it isn't the same thing at all. She just doesn't understand.

Recently there has been quite a flurry of activity on the telephone, far into the night on one occasion. George had the audacity to take another girl out! Shock, horror, how COULD he do exactly what Jenny is doing and expect to get away with it? In fact, I gather that George is not having a regular liaison, including mouth-to-mouth contact, with anyone else. But it appears that while Jenny can carry on with Dirk and it means nothing, George only has to talk to another girl and it's a betrayal.

I couldn't resist asking Jenny, during one of her many rants on the subject, what exactly the difference was between George and Jasmine and Jenny and Dirk. Was it perhaps that George had only been seen with Jasmine once, whilst Jenny and Dirk were together all the time? Or was it perhaps that George smiled and talked, while Jenny only cuddled, held hands and snogged in Dirk's father's car? (That certainly shut her up – they won't be parking outside the house under the lamp any more!)

Jenny spluttered for a while, and then claimed I simply did not understand. She did not, of course, answer the question, but swept from the room looking very dignified and hard-done-by. Isn't it amazing how much we parents do not understand?

Sadie will be here next week! I can't wait for some intelligent company. Not to mention all the latest news about what's going on at home. I have asked Sadie to keep a special eye on Louise Ann Maynard and also on Jasmine, but I don't think Jasmine is much of a threat now I have had time to think about it. She is a good friend, and wouldn't do the dirty on me. Not like Louise

Ann Maynard – whether or not she fancies Jack J. Jackson is beside the point for her.

I am getting a bit fed up with the company of my family. It's so unrelenting. We are together all day and all evening. The only time I get away from them is when I go out somewhere with Dirk, and then Mum gets all quiet and gives me a horrible look when I come home, so it's hardly worth it. Dad is working all the time, Lizzie babbles constantly but says absolutely nothing except an occasional mum-mum and dad-dad (which she says to trees, people and flowers as well as all her toys). Jon doesn't stop asking questions or pestering me to do things with him, and that leaves Mum, who witters on about culture, history, scenery etc. as though she really thinks I'm interested in all these places she keeps dragging us off to.

I am cultured up to the eyeballs. I have history pouring out of my ears and beautiful scenery stacked up in my memory bank to last well into the next century. ENOUGH! I JUST WANT TO BE LEFT ALONE. Why do I have to play the jolly daughter all the time? I'd far rather stay in bed than be dragged round some of these 'attractions' she dreams up for my entertainment.

28th July

We visited the historic Craigdarrach Castle today – a beautiful Victorian mansion in Victoria. There is very little architectural history in Canada and this building, though not old by British standards, is considered very old and much respected here in Victoria. I thought Jenny would be able to soak up some of the atmosphere, but she shrugged her shoulders and said it was just an old house, why make such a fuss about it?

I will be very glad to see her friend Sadie, who arrives in a few days. Maybe she and Jenny will stay behind sometimes when we go out, if our destination is not to their liking. I wish Jenny would stay behind sometimes. I'd far rather she sat and vegetated in front of the TV than cast cynical and dismissive comments over everything the little ones and I enjoy doing. But she has been making real efforts to join in, so I don't like to discourage her by asking her not to come along. If only she had a few topics of conversation other than herself, George, and Dirk.

3rd August

Sadie got here yesterday. It seems a whole lifetime since I saw her in England. She said the flight was really long and lonely. When I asked her whether there had been any decent looking boys, she said she didn't know. She hadn't even checked. Wow! That must be true love. It makes me feel a bit bad that I didn't want to introduce her to Dirk. She did take David Slater away from me, but now she has Adam, she has eyes only for him, as they say in novels. That is so sweet.

We talked almost right through the night, and Sadie fell asleep in the end, in the middle of telling me all the news from home. I'll have to catch up on it tomorrow. One thing she did tell me is that Louise Ann Maynard and Jack J. Jackson are indeed going out together. It's one of those well-known secrets around school. Sadie says that the Head has talked to them both about it and warned them to be discreet. Although the maneater is over sixteen and anyway they're not sleeping together (they say), Jackson could still be in danger of a charge of unprofessional conduct! Sadie was told all this by Louise herself, apparently, at a youth centre disco. I don't call that very discreet. Still, Jack J. Jackson deserves anything that's coming. I can't think of a couple of people better suited to each other than those two.

Cathy and Ted have split up. Sadie doesn't know all

the details, but she thinks it was Cathy who finished it. She has gone back to her house, which isn't going to be sold now. She doesn't have a job any more, either. She got the sack, but Sadie doesn't know why. We tried to telephone her but then we remembered the phone was disconnected when the house was left empty. Poor Cathy. We both feel completely useless, wanting to help but not having any idea how to.

4th August

Sadie arrived yesterday; she will be staying for two weeks and hopefully will keep Jenny cheerful and prevent a lot of whingeing. After the hugs and squeals at the airport when they were reunited, they immediately started talking, and haven't stopped yet although more than 24 hours have passed. Sadie looks like a zombie but is determined not to give in to the ten hour time difference. You have to admire her pluck, even though she is almost at the stage of propping her eyelids open with matchsticks.

Things are going well for Mike at the moment and he is able to ease off a bit, so the timing is perfect. While we have Sadie and Mike with us we are going to do the most exciting activities from our list. We will be watching for whales, and visiting the rain forest up island, among other things. It will be a true holiday. And, fortunately, no room in the car for Dirk on his days off...

7th August

Sadie and I have been mooching about on our own for the last couple of days, letting the olds go their own way. We even, very nobly, babysat for a couple of evenings. Dad has finally been let loose from work for a few days

122

and they went out to dinner. Last night they went to some gruesome classical concert down at the harbour. It ended with fireworks, apparently. Isn't that a bit wasteful, with a geriatric audience?

Dirk took us to Sooke, to the pot holes, yesterday. I didn't want Sadie to miss seeing them. She thought Sooke was great, but I don't think she likes Dirk very much. She was very quiet when we got back. When I asked her what she thought of him she just said, 'He's nice enough', and changed the subject. I suppose seeing us together reminds her of how much she is missing Adam. He has telephoned twice already (which is more than George has done in over two months!).

8th August

Having Sadie here has been even more of a break than I hoped. Not only is she keeping Jenny well occupied but the two of them have even looked after Jon and Lizzie to give Mike and me a break, which has been very welcome.

Mike is so much more relaxed now that things have sorted themselves out at work. He is ahead of schedule, and these few days holiday will be even more enjoyable for him now. Last night we went to a wonderful open-air concert at the harbour. Moonlight over the water, boats bobbing under coloured lights, and beautiful music – a magnificent experience. To top it all, the evening ended with fireworks actually synchronised with the music. The combination was stunning. I tried to describe it to Jon but he couldn't see the point of fireworks for old people and felt quite aggrieved that we had left him at home.

It is interesting to see that Sadie does not like the situation between Jenny and Dirk any more than I do. She has said nothing, as far as I am aware, but you can tell by the way she looks at him that she is

*uncomfortable. I hope she manages to talk some
sense into Jenny.*

10th August

Today we went on an expedition to spot whales offshore
around the gulf islands. It was brilliant. We had to wear
huge yellow coveralls with hoods and looked like
something from another planet. But I survived the blue
plastic mac experience at Niagara, and nothing could be
as humiliating as that.

We left Lizzie with a family a couple of doors down
that Mum has made friends with and at first she was
fussing all the time about whether she would be all right.
But Dad managed to convince her that since this family
has four much older kids and the mother is a nurse – and
they're all besotted with Lizzie – she would spend the
afternoon being played with and pandered to and
generally very well looked after. Jon made a remarkably
witty (for him) joke about her having a whale of a time
just like us. And he didn't keep repeating it after we'd
laughed. He is growing up at last.

Anyway, we put on these awful yellow suits and set
forth in an inflatable dinghy. It was great whenever a
bigger boat came near us – the wash made our boat
jump like a fairground ride. Sadie and I kept telling the
pilot to ride into the waves, but Mum looked a bit green
at the end so we had pity on her. We saw loads of birds
and seals on the rocky little islands, and followed a
school of porpoises. They seemed to enjoy having an
audience, and were whizzing round us, underneath the
boat, and jumping into the air as though they were
putting on a private show. Best of all, just as we were
giving up hope, we saw the whales. They heaved
themselves into the air several times while all the people
in the boat scrabbled desperately for the cameras, and
then disappeared. Sadie actually cried; she said it was

the most beautiful experience of her entire life. It was pretty moving. We took loads and loads of photographs, trying to get shots of the porpoises and the whales leaving the water – don't know how successful we were, but it doesn't matter. I'll never forget the sight.

Sadie just had to telephone Adam as soon as we got back to tell him all about it, so she dragged me off to the call box. Listening to her describing it all to Adam made me ache for George. I have been missing him much more than I realized. I have tried to take my mind off him with Dirk, but there's no room in my heart for anyone else. I am so glad Dirk and I haven't got more involved than just holiday romance kissy sort of stuff. Dirk sometimes forgets our agreement and tries for a bit more, but however tempted I am I never get carried away. Sadie and Adam are completely in tune with each other. They don't need anyone or anything else. That's how it should be for George and me.

I telephoned George but he was at work. Alicia sounded really pleased to hear from me, though. She said George was thoroughly miserable and was marking the days off the kichen wall calendar until I came home. That made me feel a) much better to know how much he misses me and b) even more guilty about Dirk.

11th August

Yesterday we took a boat trip out to do some wildlife watching. It was a fantastic experience and one we will all remember. We saw seals, cormorants, a whole variety of seabirds, porpoises and orca whales. They are very picturesque, though small by whale standards, and everyone on the boat was very excited. Jon did not stop talking about it all evening, and Sadie and Jenny had to dash straight off to the callbox to tell their men all about it, too. Sadie insists on calling Adam from a callbox so as not to run up a phone bill for us. I cannot persuade her that she could just as easily pay us for any calls she has made. Perhaps she just wants to talk in private. I must say she and Adam seem a perfect match – sensible, down-to-earth and devoted to each other. I think Jenny is having serious thoughts about her relationship with George. She has spent more time writing letters and has also called him more since Sadie has been here. I hope this means Dirk is fading from the scene.

I had a long letter from Cathy this morning. She and Ted have split up and Cathy has left her job because he kept popping in to the bank to try and get her to change her mind. Poor Cathy; her life seems to be one trauma after another. Ted did his best to help her after her mother's death but his own unresolved problems made it very difficult for them both. Cathy says she finally realized that there was no long term future in their relationship and it could only get more painful. She also says that she recognizes how much of her childhood was lost in all the problems of living with an alcoholic mother, and how easily she is trapped in bad relationships because anything seems better than having nothing.

It was a very mature, very moving letter. Cathy says she has decided to go back to school and try to get her 'A' levels and a university place. She is hoping to do a teaching or nursing degree to give her life more direction and purpose. She has gone back to the family home, but reading between the lines she seems desperately lonely. Mike and I have talked it over and decided to offer Cathy a home with us for as long as she needs it. If she does go back to school it will be very difficult for her to cope with studying and running a home. So I have written tonight to suggest she moves in with us and rents out her house until she has finished school and university. I hope she accepts; it worked out all right before when she lived with us during Gloria's bad times. I know Jenny won't mind, *but I haven't said anything to her about Cathy. I will wait to see what Cathy's reaction is.*

Today we spent the whole day, and most of the evening, in the company of trees. We drove right to the top of the Island – it took nearly three hours – to visit the rain forest. It sounded dead romantic and mystical, but it was very boring. Tree after tree after tree, and nowhere to stop for the loo or a drink, never mind a decent hamburger bar. I'm all for saving the world, and I think the chopping and logging and clearing that's going on is scandalous. But I don't think the general look of a forest is very damaged by a small roadside cafe.

By the time we got to civilisation – a place named Quequelot – Sadie and I were desperate for food. Jon and Lizzie had given up hope and gone to sleep. We stopped at the strangest cafe I have ever been in. There was a bowling alley inside, with a restaurant area beside it, and a milk bar serving milk shakes and ice creams. At the back there was a room full of snooker and pool tables. It was just like an old movie. The food was good, though. Afterwards we went for a walk through the forest – yet more trees – and I have to admit the size of some of the trees was pretty incredible. They were so huge you couldn't see the tops of them, and even if we all joined hands we would never stretch around the trunks. Mum kept going on about the majestic peace and beauty of it all. We very kindly did not share with Mum the posters Jon showed to Sadie and me in the car park, warning people to keep young children close and pointing out that wild cougars were in the forests and were attracted by the sound of children's voices. Another poster warned what to do if a bear came up to you! We agreed that the whole trip would have been far less boring if we'd had the opportunity to fight off a cougar. If we'd known about bears being attracted to food we could have taken some bread along with us. Maybe we'll get the chance another time.

We ended the day at Tofino, watching the aquaplanes take off and land while Lizzie gurgled away on the sand and Jon made intricate patterns with stones on the beach. It was a good day.

15th August

Another highlight of our time in Canada today – the temperate rain forests in the north of the island. They are so beautiful, so timeless and majestic. You can almost feel the peace and harmony dropping from the branches; it really is quite mystical. It was a very fitting way to end Sadie's holiday with us. Tomorrow she travels home, and we have only about two weeks more before we must do the same. Time has flown and we have had a the trip of a lifetime, but in many ways it will be good to get back.

Jenny and Sadie tried hard not to be swayed by the romance and beauty of the rainforests, but I know it got to them just as it did to me. The experience was perhaps a little tempered for me by the paragraph in the guide book about taking care not to attract cougars or bears – I love wildlife, but not the idea of things with teeth, claws and a temper coming near my children! I didn't mention this to the children of course; it would have frightened them out of their wits, and spoilt an otherwise beautiful experience. So I bore the brunt of anxiety alone. I found out afterwards that really we were quite safe. Cougar attacks are rare, and bears will leave you alone unless you aggravate them. (So I'm told, anyway. Thankfully, I had no chance to test the theory...)

Sadie went home today. It was brill having her here, and she's taken back a bundle of letters and cards and some Canadian candies for my George. We very nearly parted as enemies over George, as it happens. I could see for a couple of days now that Sadie has been trying to keep something in. You can always tell with Sadie. She goes very quiet, and you sometimes catch her looking at you as though she's trying to read your mind. It's hopeless to ever try and get anything out of her, though, until she's ready. I don't think she even knows she's in this mood when she has it.

In the end, she asked if she could tell me something that was on her mind and I said yes, of course. The something that has been on her mind was that ever since she clapped eyes on Dirk she has disliked him. She said he was a real poser and she couldn't understand why I would want someone with a fake tan, permed hair and an ego problem when I could have the genuine article (George). I said I still had George, and it wasn't the same thing at all. She said I was being unfaithful to George, and it's cruel to string him along when I'm clearly going after Dirk as well. I was horrified and said Dirk was just a friend, not serious like George. Then she REALLY blew her stack and said in that case I was stringing DIRK along, and she knew what kind of girl THAT made me. She didn't actually say the word but I could see it burning on her brain. I was so shocked I slapped her on the cheek – not hard, but it was a terrible thing to do, and I started crying when I realized. So did Sadie. So we ended up friends, but the atmosphere was still a bit difficult when she left.

I stayed awake most of the night thinking about some of the things she said. I know she's right. I don't want to admit it or to look at myself the way she (and presumably others) must see me, but I have been stupid and I have been unfair to George. I don't deserve for him to love

129

me, but I know he does. How could I even think about risking that to get rid of a bit of loneliness? I don't know what I'm going to say to Dirk, but I've got to find a way out of this mess.

Sadie and Jenny had a mega row last night. You could hear them all over the house, even though they were in the basement. Afterwards they both behaved as if everything was fine and no-one volunteered any information, so I didn't ask. Jon was out with the neighbours, which was a pity. He would just have asked outright what was going on or, better still, hung around outside Jenny's door and caught the drift of the conversation. He would have charged me for the information, I expect, but at least I would have some idea what sparked this row off. Sadie seemed to be getting the upper hand. I wonder if it's anything to do with George, or Dirk? It's very frustrating when your children get too old to tell you every last detail of their lives.

Mum has started shopping again, so we must be revving up for the homeward journey. She decided to do some Christmas shopping while we were here. Christmas! She is such an embarrassment. I pointed out that half the people she buys presents for could be DEAD by Christmas. She just said if that happened there would be more to worry about than having wasted a few pounds. I went out with her a couple of times, but even I couldn't stay the pace she sets when she gets going. I looked after the kids.

Dirk has asked me out to dinner – a last farewell, he

says – tomorrow. He's going back to college to get his books and papers sorted out before the next semester begins. That was quite a relief. Neither one of us wants to carry on being anything more than casual friends, and although I will be sad to say goodbye I know it's for the best. He isn't the man for me, and George is too precious to risk throwing away.

I called George tonight, to tell him to go round Sadie's and get his parcel. I know Sadie won't mention Dirk, and I intend never to speak about him after tomorrow night. He will simply be a shadow of the past.

24th August

Dinner with Dirk was awful. AWFUL. I can't think about it without squirming inside. I thought it was going to be a laugh, a last light-hearted bit of fun before we went our separate ways. But before we had even got halfway through our Dairy Queen Special he started telling me how his friend's parents were away and his friend had said we could go there if we wanted. I thought he meant to go and keep the friend company and watch a video or something, but the way he kept going on made me feel uncomfortable. When we got there, the house was in darkness. Dirk pulled a key out of his pocket and let us in. When I asked where his friend was he laughed and said to stop playing the innocent, I'd made it perfectly clear what I really wanted! I was so shocked for a moment I couldn't even speak. Then I asked him what he meant. He said he 'knew English girls took a while to warm up', that it had been fun going slow for a change, but this would be my last chance to find out what it was like to 'go with someone who really knew their stuff'.

He was so sure of himself, and suddenly I saw myself the way he saw me – young, stupid and leading him on. I tried to tell him he had got it all wrong, but he was all over me and I had to push him off! I mentioned George and he laughed. He said George sounded pathetic.

It was awful. Humiliating. When I said I was really sorry if he thought we were more than just good friends, he looked at me in astonishment. He said why on earth would he want a silly little schoolgirl for a friend? He said he had never done it with an English girl and thought it would be 'a laugh'. He thought I was just playing hard to get, or feeling a bit nervous because George was all I knew. In other words, I suppose, I was worried about how I would cope with a real man, like him!

I just don't want to remember any of this, but his face won't leave my mind. When I said I wasn't interested, he couldn't believe it. He looked at me as if I was a slut, then he just left and slammed the door – just left me, on the other side of town in a strange country late at night. All this time I thought we were friends, and he was only after another statistic to brag about with the boys. Even though I had no idea where I was, I didn't follow him. I couldn't bear the idea of getting into a car with him.

I had to telephone home, there was no other choice. Dad was so calm, even when I said I didn't know where I was. I was crying so hard I couldn't even speak properly. He said to see if there were any envelopes or anything lying around with the address on. I found one in the kitchen, but I was terrifiied the house owners would come back and think I was a burglar. Dad said he would come as quickly as he could, and told me to wait inside the house, but I couldn't. I stood outside in the dark, with all these spooky bushes and no street lights, and it seemed like hours before he came. I just fell into the car and cried all the way home. Dad asked if Dirk had done anything to me. When I said no, he said thank God but he would probably kill him anyway. Then he shut up and drove, too fast, so I could see he was upset.

Mum was as white as a sheet until she knew I was O.K. She kept asking if I was all right, or if I needed to talk. I told her everything. It was a double humiliation going through it all again and admitting that she had been right about Dirk all along. But it wasn't fair not to be honest with her. She said she was scared out of her wits when I called Dad, worrying about what had happened to me. She said she knew now that she should have put a stop to me seeing Dirk ages ago, and she feels bad that she let it go on even though she had a strong feeling that he was bad news.

I just feel awful. Mum couldn't have done anything. I wouldn't have listened, and anything she had done to try and stop me seeing Dirk would only have made me want to see him more. I hate myself for hurting her and Dad. It's made a miserable end to what should have been a wonderful holiday. Mum had to grab Dad to stop him going next door right there and then to give Dirk a hiding; I've never seen him so angry. It's me he should have been angry with, not Dirk. I thought I could have it all. I liked flirting with Dirk, and I used him to fill the gap left by George and make myself feel a bit more experienced for when I got home. Perhaps Sadie was right about me.

Mum and Dad sat up with me almost all night, talking. They made me feel a lot better about what had happened, and were so understanding. Dad said it was a simple case of crossed wires, and nothing to spoil my life over. But I can't help feeling it's all my fault.

24th August

Jenny got her come-uppance with Dirk, in a big way tonight. He took her out for what she thought was going to be a lighthearted farewell dinner and found that he had a big seduction scene all planned. Jenny seems not to have had any inkling that this was going to happen. She's not as streetwise as she likes to think. Dirk clearly thought he and Jenny were heading in a totally different direction. It could have ended a lot nastier than it did. Dirk didn't attack

Jenny but he did accuse her of leading him on and then he just dumped her miles away in a strange house and drove off. Mike and I were astounded when she telephoned home to ask if he would come and get her – she didn't even know where she was! The poor girl had to root through a complete stranger's house to find something with an address on it. Dirk is one of life's smoothies, and he'll be with another girl before Jenny's even unpacked her cases. But Jenny will carry the humiliation of tonight for a long time. Mike is furious with Dirk for leaving her like that, but I persuaded him that it would be pointless to confront Dirk. He behaved badly, but he didn't hurt Jenny anywhere except in her pride. I don't believe for one moment that Jenny consciously strung Dirk along, and the humiliation must have been awful. We didn't need to say anything to her; she realizes now, too late, what I've been trying to tell her all along about how easily things can get out of hand. Maybe that's a lesson well learned.

31st August

We have been packing and cleaning up all day, ready for the flight home tomorrow. This house has become a real home to us in the last four months, and I will miss it. And the neighbours. And the balmy summer weather. And the smiling, friendly faces of people. And the shops. And the lovely big roads. Sometimes I think I could live here for ever. But we have another home, our proper one, and that calls to me as well. We have had a wonderful time here, and the children have all grown up enormously. They are all bronzed and healthy and full of life. Jon and Lizzie have filled out a bit and Jon has shot up – Mum will hardly recognize him. Mike has done a very good job and has been heaped with praise, so he looks very bright-eyed *and bushy-tailed. Jenny seems to have matured quite a lot in her time here, particularly since that awful night with Dirk. The gawkish teenage edges have been rubbed into smoother curves, and she has begun to get to grips with the responsibilities of adult life. And me? I have had a lovely, lazy time having all the best bits of full-time motherhood without the lonely drudgery. I feel younger, fitter, and ready for whatever Jenny, Jon and Lizzie have to throw at me once we get back.*

Dirk went back to college a couple of days ago. He told his mother he needed to get some study done before the new semester started. She has no idea about what happened, and even told Jenny she hoped they would keep in touch. Jenny was very good: she smiled and said something politely non-committal. Afterwards she told me that she didn't feel so angry with Dirk any more, or even bad about herself. She just accepted that she had simply been too young and inexperienced for Dirk, and there had been misunderstanding on both sides. Now that's what I call mature. She and Cathy and Sadie have all grown up so fast this last year. They are taking charge of their lives and shaping their futures in a way that would have been impossible in my day at their age. I feel quite envious.

August 31st

I can't believe we're going home tomorrow. HOME! GEORGE!! He's trying to change his ward shift so that he can come and meet me. I'll be devastated if he's not there. I'm going to plant my lips on his and let them take root there. I am never, ever, going to go away from him again or let him get away from me.

The neighbours all came over for a farewell drink this evening. Dirk's back in Ottawa now. His mum said she telephoned him yesterday, and he sent his love 'to everybody'. I think she was fishing for information, but I didn't give her any. I don't want to think about Dirk any more. That part of my life is over, and there's no point going over it. Besides, how can I tell Dirk's proud and doting mother that her lovely son is a creep? Mum was right all along about him.

Cathy is going to meet us at the airport as well. She called Mum last night and they talked for ages. Mum has said Cathy can live with us for a while. She's going to be coming back to school. She'll be in the year below me and Sadie, which will be weird, but she sounds determined to get herself together. I'm not sure how I'll cope with her in the family again for what looks like a very long time, but I agree with Mum that we have to do this. I cannot imagine what my life would be like if I had no-one looking out for me. I don't appreciate everything I've got, and I take Mum and Dad for granted, but I'm so glad they are who they are and I am who I am.

I've just read that last bit and I think it's obvious I had a bit too much farewell wine. I'd better go to bed!

3rd September

Will someone please explain to my body that we are in a different country now? We got back at ten a.m. English time, but to our bodies it was midnight. Mine still hasn't recovered. It is 4 a.m. and I have had to get up and have something to eat, because I'm wide awake. I met Dad in the kitchen – he was making a meal for Lizzie! She has no idea what time it is at all, and beamed like mad when she saw me. I played with her for a while and then Mum got up, so I went back to bed. Jon seems the only one who doesn't mind the time change. He was a bit tired on the first day, but apart from that he can't see what all the fuss is about, and goes about with this cheery expression that makes you want to kill him.

I am so glad to be home, I just go around the house touching things and saying hello to them with a soppy grin. George was at the airport with a huge bunch of flowers and I was so overjoyed to see him I thought I would cry. We talked and talked and kissed until our lips were sore. We have seen each other for every available minute. How could I ever have doubted that he was the one for me? He's all I ever want.

I returned home to big news. Sadie and Adam are engaged! They plan to get married next September, before they go to university. They are both applying to the same ones, so they should be O.K. If one gets a place and one doesn't, they'll still get married and the other one will work for a year and try again. They've got it all planned. Sadie says her mum is not very keen on them marrying this young, but she said since she'd nearly lost Sadie last year when she was so ill it was difficult to deny her anything. Sadie's mum is usually even more old fashioned than mine on that kind of thing. It was a real surprise. Sadie and Adam are very sensible about it all. It's hard to believe they'll end up as one of those divorce statistics for people who married young. I hope not. I am going to be chief bridesmaid, and George will be best man. I have only been a bridesmaid once, for my cousin, and I know Sadie would not dream of putting me in the naff sort of clothes I had to wear then, so it'll be great.

I actually saw Louise Ann Maynard on the arm of our illustrious teacher, Jack J. Jackson, this morning. They were crossing the street in town. Louise gave me a cheery wave as if we were the best of friends and they sauntered off arm in arm into Tesco's. I don't call that very discreet. Next term should be a lot of fun. I must talk to Sadie about how we can maximise the entertainment value there.

I have told George all about Dirk. Well, nearly all. I couldn't bear to have dark secrets from him, not since I've decided he's likely to be the one I'll spend the rest of my life with. Also, Mum pointed out that Jon is almost bound to say something. George didn't like to hear it, but he understands that I have learned from the experience, and he forgives me. Now that we are back together after such a long time apart, we feel even more strongly that we want to be together. I think we both know, though, that neither one of us has the courage of Sadie and Adam to say yes, definitely, the rest of my life I will always feel this way.

I didn't want to go to Canada but I'm glad I did. Being that far from home and from everything that felt familiar made me stand back and take a good look at what I want from life. I want George, but it would be wrong to marry. I need to know that if another Dirk comes along I'll handle it without getting in too deep. Also, Sadie doesn't want anything or anyone except Adam and she seems very sure she'll never change her mind. I think it's great to feel that way, but I don't, not yet. When I look at their life together, what strikes me most of all is that they don't have much fun. It's a comfortable, settled kind of love. I want change, excitement, FUN. I want to travel and see lots of other countries and cultures. I want to get a career, achieve something important and be independent for a while before I settle down with someone and have forevermore to compromise or ask another person if what I want to do is all right with him.

Maybe I'll have all that and George too, or maybe we will end up wanting to go different ways. I know now I haven't finished growing up yet – that came as a surprise, because I always thought I was so mature.

Whatever happens George will be that very special person who taught me what real love is all about. I hope we always stay together, but if we don't I hope we can always be friends. I will always be happy to have known him.

These are all very grown-up statements. I hope I haven't matured too much. This year will be the last opportunity for Sadie and me to be young, footloose and free before she becomes an old married lady and I...what will I be doing this time next year? I have absolutely no idea. So it's important to make this year the most fun-packed ever. I would hate to develop a conscience about all the little embarrassments I have planned for Louise Ann Maynard and her dashing young teacher for next term...